'You!' Penny exclaimed in horror.

'You know damn well it's me,' Dare snapped. 'Why else would you have bothered travelling all this way? Well, you've wasted your time chasing after me,' he continued before she had time to marshal her thoughts. 'I've got no time in my life for empty-headed debutantes with no morals and no ambition, so you can just turn around and go straight back to England.'

'Can't,' she retorted shortly, spitting the single word out through gritted teeth. If she'd needed a reminder of why she'd loathed this narrow-minded man from the first time they'd spoken, he'd just given it to her.

Josie Metcalfe lives in Cornwall now with her long-suffering husband, four children and two horses, but, as an army brat frequently on the move, books became the only friends who came with her wherever she went. Now that she writes them herself she is making new friends, and hates saying goodbye at the end of a book—but there are always more characters in her head clamouring for attention until she can't wait to tell their stories.

A LITTLE BIT
OF MAGIC

BY
JOSIE METCALFE

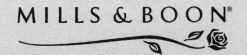
MILLS & BOON®

*MILLS & BOON and MILLS & BOON with the Rose Device
are registered trademarks of the publisher.*

*First published in Great Britain 1997
Harlequin Mills & Boon Limited,
Eton House, 18-24 Paradise Road, Richmond, Surrey TW9 1SR*

© Josie Metcalfe 1997

ISBN 0 263 80772 X

*Set in Times 11 on 11½ pt. by
Rowland Phototypesetting Limited
Bury St Edmunds, Suffolk*

03-9804-47932-D

*Printed and bound in Great Britain
by Mackays of Chatham PLC, Chatham.*

AUTHOR'S NOTE

MERLIN (Medical Emergency Relief International) is a British medical charity, providing emergency relief in crisis zones worldwide.

It sends volunteer medical and support personnel to assist during the first phases of disasters when local services have broken down and people are at their most vulnerable. MERLIN is on call twenty-four hours a day and can respond to a crisis anywhere in the world within seventy-two hours—from Azerbaijan to Zaire and every letter of the alphabet in between.

CHAPTER ONE

'TRAFFIC!' Penny muttered as she slung the strap of her shoulder-bag over the arm of the chair before she flopped down into its twin with a sigh of relief. 'An hour and a half to do a thirty-minute journey. . .'

She knew it was her own choice to live so far away from the hospital, but the crowded streets surrounding the elderly buildings where she worked in the specially converted TB unit were so depressing that she'd always thought the journey to her bright modern flat worthwhile—until today.

Automatically, one hand reached out to press the replay button on her answering machine, and she heard the tape click and whir as it rewound.

She screwed her eyes up tight, pressing her head back hard against the squashy upholstery and superstitiously crossing her fingers.

The one thing that she was hoping *not* to hear was Ian's voice. When would he get the message?

She'd told the handsome young registrar when he'd first asked her out that she wasn't interested in starting a relationship with him. Unfortunately, in spite of the fact that she'd refused every one of his invitations, it didn't seem to have deterred his persistence. Even though he'd now moved to another hospital for the next stage of his training, he still kept ringing to leave invitations on—

'Hello, Penelope, dear. Are you there. . .?'

Her mother's distinctive cut-glass accent dismissed her exasperated thoughts about Ian, replacing them with an immediate surge of apprehension—the strange mix of guilt, frustration and anger which always overwhelmed her whenever she heard from one of her parents.

'Just a reminder that we'll be there to collect you at six-thirty. The reception for MERLIN starts at seven for seven-thirty, and we *mustn't* be late. . .' There was a pause as if her mother was trying to decide whether to say anything more, before she continued, 'I hope you're going to wear your pretty blue dress—'

Her voice was cut off abruptly by the machine as she ran out of time and the tape whirred as it rewound again, but Penny was too busy grabbing for her bag to notice, her fingers frantically scrabbling through the jumble of contents in the bottom as she tried to unearth her diary.

'Not tonight,' she begged as she flicked through the pages. 'Please, not tonight.'

She groaned, and was conscious that her shoulders slumped when she read the brief note scribbled across the page, confirming that she *had* agreed to accompany her parents to their company's corporate fundraiser tonight.

There had been so much tension between herself and her parents ever since she'd begun her nursing training that when her mother had asked her to attend Penny had quickly accepted, looking on it as some small way to begin repairing the bridges between them.

The fact that the charity they were raising money for was one of her own personal favourites had been an additional inducement, but as for wearing the 'pretty blue dress' her mother had suggested. . .

Penny shuddered at the thought.

It didn't matter that the gown in question was a designer original which had cost a fortune, nor did it help that the many yards of gossamer-fine pure silk would probably have looked wonderful and ethereal on an anorexic six-foot-tall teenage debutante with a year-round tan.

Unfortunately, *she* was barely five feet four, and although she was slender she still possessed the normal number of curves for a twenty-six-year-old woman so on her it looked much more like a ghastly electric-blue meringue.

She glanced up at the small clock on the mantlepiece as she distractedly tucked the escaping strands of her long blonde hair behind her ear. When her eyes actually focused on the time her fingers stiffened in horror.

'Half an hour?' she shrieked as she catapulted out of her chair and leapt towards the bathroom in outright panic, kicking off her shoes as she went and fumbling at the fastenings of her clothes.

She knew that the infallibly punctual Wilson would have set off in his beloved Vanden Plas at least ten minutes ago so it was already too late to phone and let her mother know she was running late. . .

'I'll never make it,' she moaned, then gasped as she dived under the shower, without waiting for the water to warm up—one hand already reaching for the bottle of shampoo. She could only afford two minutes but she didn't dare to skip her usual liberal application of conditioner or her naturally curly hair would never allow itself to be subdued.

Every second of the ritual seemed to take for ever, her hands fumbling every task from turning off the water to tangling the towel and plugging in the hairdryer.

'More haste, less speed,' she muttered as she tried to blow her hair dry at the same time as she scrabbled through her drawer for clean underwear.

Somewhere in the depths there was a pair of flesh-coloured panties she'd bought specifically to go under the dress she'd chosen to wear tonight.

Her hands paused in their tasks and a brief smile curved her lips as she glanced at the garment hanging in solitary splendour on the back of the bedroom door.

It was one her parents hadn't seen before—a stunningly simple white dress with a sophisticated Grecian appearance in the bared shoulder and fluted full-length draping of the fine flowing silk.

When her mother had initially extended the invitation for this evening's event Penny had actually contemplated going back home to choose one of the formal dresses she'd left behind when she'd moved into her own flat, but when she'd remembered the selection she had to choose from she realised that this would be the first formal event she'd attended since she'd left home.

Suddenly it had seemed important that she should go out and choose a new dress to celebrate her independence, in spite of the fact that her salary would be hard-pressed to stretch that far, and she'd been delighted with her eventual choice.

The diagonally draped bodice was cleverly constructed so that she didn't need to wear a bra underneath it, but she'd realised the first time she'd tried the dress on that her usual panties would show through the fine fabric like a neon signpost—hence the purchase of the elusive underwear. . .

'I haven't got time for this,' she groaned as she upended the drawer on her bed and pawed futilely through the resulting muddle.

At intervals over the next fifteen minutes she searched again, between sweeping her hair up into a swift coil and spearing it with a handful of pins to hold it in place and applying the fastest make-up in her life.

Not for the first time did she thank her grand-mother's Russian genes for giving that slightly exotic tilt to her eyes and endowing her cheek-bones with their sculpted height and shape.

She stepped back from the mirror just long enough to realise that her hasty hairdo was less than secure. Several tendrils were already escaping to curl around her face and against her neck in an accidental imitation of the artful disarray achieved by the daughters of some of her parent's socialite friends.

'Well, there isn't time to do it again,' she grumbled as she turned back to the jumble of clothing on the bed.

She still hadn't found the elusive panties when there was a sharp ring on her doorbell and she had to stifle a shriek of frustration.

'Just coming,' she promised into the safety inter-com, knowing that there was no way her parents would tolerate being kept waiting outside.

The two of them already disapproved of her choice of career and where she lived, and if this evening wasn't going to start off with a lecture on poor time-keeping she had to go straight out and join them *now*.

'I'll just have to go without,' she declared aloud, and heard the echo of hysteria in her voice as she thrust her feet into waiting gold sandals.

What other choice did she have? She thought as one hand grabbed her evening bag and matching silk wrap while the other scooped up the small pile of jewellery she'd left ready. She'd have to put it on in the car. . .

A playful breeze stirred the semi-translucent fabric against her body as she stepped out onto the front path. She suddenly felt very vulnerable as she realised exactly how little she was wearing, and pulled the silky wrap more tightly around her shoulders.

'Good evening, Wilson,' she said brightly as she slid into the passenger seat, hoping she'd managed to keep the relief out of her voice when she realised that so far he was the only one in the car. 'Are we picking my parents up on the way?'

'No, miss. Your mother had to go in early—some problem with the catering or the seating arrangements, I believe.'

His expression was wry as he shot a swift glance at her under his prominent grey eyebrows, and she couldn't help laughing aloud.

'When is there ever not a problem with the caterers?' she demanded in a voice full of resignation for the familiar situation, and she felt her tension easing as she shared the time-worn joke about her mother's perfectionism with the man who seemed to have been part of her life since for ever.

'Or was it the florists, or the musicians. . .?' he continued in his courtly-sounding voice.

'Musicians?' Penny squeaked. 'Oh, Wilson, no! That means the dratted evening is going to go on for ever, and I've got to go to work tomorrow!'

'Well, miss, look on the bright side—at least it should mean that there'll be more money collected for the charity.'

'That's going to be small consolation in the morning when I'm nursing sore toes and fighting to keep my eyes open!'

Wilson chuckled richly and the sound reminded Penny of the many times she'd wished that the kindly man was related to her—there was something about his down-to-earth common sense that reminded her of her beloved grandmother.

She pressed her lips together as she felt again the pang of loss.

It was nearly six years ago that the sprightly old lady had died, but Penny still missed her dreadfully. She had been a treasured ally against her parents when she'd been battling to be allowed to start her nursing training, delighting in another opportunity to dent Sir Gregory's air of invincibility—as if it hadn't been enough that she steadfastly refused to admit that she spoke or understood anything but her Russian mother tongue. . .

The thoughts of her grandmother reminded her that she hadn't yet donned the precious items of jewellery which the wickedly indomitable old woman had bequeathed to her, and she twisted open the clasp on her bag and delved inside.

The sleek golden links of the necklace slipped through her fingers as she sought the clasp and encircled her neck with it, the cool weight warming swiftly against her skin as she checked that the diamonds set in the central links were lying correctly.

'Rose-cut diamonds,' she could hear her grandmother saying as she'd shown the beautiful jewellery to her. 'They don't cut them that way any more, but when your grandfather gave them to me. . .' Her eyes had taken on that familiar far-away look and she'd smiled softly to herself as she'd told the story of the gift from the czar to her wide-eyed granddaughter.

'Your grandfather was a gardener in the gardens at Peterhof, near St Petersburg, where the royal family was living. Alexis was the first male heir born to a reigning czar since the seventeenth century, and when the young czarevich fell my Gregor scooped him up in his arms and carried him in to get help. . .'

Her grandmother had explained that the czar's precious heir had suffered from haemophilia which he had inherited through his grandmother, Queen Victoria.

At that time there had been no medical treatment for the condition so that a bad fall could have caused bleeding severe enough to threaten his life.

The generous gift of such beautiful jewellery in recompense for her grandfather's swift action had seemed only too believable to a young girl impressionable enough to believe in fairy-tale princes. . .

The matching bracelet gleamed against her slender wrist in the waning light of the April evening as she reached inside her little evening bag to take out the final piece of the set—the delicately crafted ring, set with a perfect single rose-cut diamond.

'They suit you,' Wilson commented quietly. 'They may be over eighty years old now, but the design suits you every bit as much as it suited your grandmother.'

'Thank you, Wilson,' she murmured through the thickness in her throat. 'You couldn't have given me a nicer compliment—in fact, those words will probably carry me right through this interminable evening!'

Her old companion made a dismissive sound, but a few minutes later he began to speak of Penny's grandmother again.

'You look like her, you know,' he said musingly. 'The colour of your hair is lighter, but your face is very similar to the photos of her at the same age.'

'Well, if I look half as beautiful as she did when I get to eighty I'll be very happy,' she murmured, touched as ever by his genuine attachment to her elderly relative.

Sometimes, when the arguments between her parents and herself had been at their worst, she'd even found herself wishing that Wilson could have been a real part of her family instead of just a lifelong employee. It would have been nice to be related to more than one person who believed in her and applauded her choices.

Now that her grandmother was gone there was no one.

'Well, here we are,' he remarked as he drew up under the *porte-cochère* of the hotel entrance, drawing her out of her introspection. 'Just you remember to bite your tongue and count to five before you speak to anyone, and you'll get through the evening!'

Penny laughed.

'I'll try, Wilson. I'll try,' she promised as she prepared to get out of the car. 'But you know what my mother can be like when she gets the bit between her teeth.'

'Very much like her daughter, in spite of the fact she isn't the one with Russian blood,' he retorted before she could close the door. 'Remember. . .count five. . .' He released the handbrake and drew away almost silently.

Penny straightened and drew in a deep breath, sending up a swift prayer for patience, before she mounted the elegant steps, conscious that another car was pulling in behind her.

Just as she reached the doors a sudden gust of wind swirled around her, and she reached up with her free hand to protect her precarious hairstyle. It was the sensation of the supple fabric of her dress pressing against the length of her body that reminded her of how utterly naked she was underneath.

She glanced back over her shoulder, hoping that the latest arrivals hadn't noticed anything untoward and feeling almost guilty for coming out so scantily clad.

There was a man behind her with one foot suspended in mid-air and an arrested expression on his handsome face as he dragged his eyes up the length of her body to meet her horrified gaze.

His eyes were a deep sapphire blue and seemed to burn into her with the intensity of a laser before a slow curl of disdain twisted his mouth and she finally managed to drag her wits together and whirl towards the door and disappear inside.

Please, God, she offered up as she hurried towards the cloakroom. Please let him just be a guest at the hotel and nothing to do with the event this evening.

She stood in front of the ornate mirror, knowing that there was very little chance of her prayers being answered. Why else would the man have been arriving dressed in impeccable evening dress if he wasn't going to attend the dinner dance?

Penny forced herself to focus on her appearance and groaned aloud when she realised just what she looked like. The breeze which had plastered her dress against her naked body had also teased out several more silky curls so that she now looked as if she'd only just climbed out of someone's bed.

She reached up to take the pins out, intending to have another attempt at securing the slippery mass, but when she saw how badly her fingers were shaking she realised that she'd better leave well enough alone.

It was as much as she could do to freshen her lipstick before she drew in a steadying breath and set off to join the growing throng, making their way towards the reception in the hotel dining room.

Surrounded by guests, her parents could do little more than frown at her but both of them pointedly glanced at their watches to let her know that she'd arrived late. Her mother spared her a pained glance when she saw that she'd ignored her suggestion about her dress, but Penny was determined not to let the constant disapproval affect her enjoyment of the evening.

It was time they realised that she had the right to make decisions of her own. . .

For nearly ten minutes she stood beside them while they greeted their guests. She concentrated on smiling as she directed each one towards the waitresses, dispensing drinks, but all the time her eyes were flickering around the room as she tried to see if he was there—tried to work out who the handsome stranger was.

Was he one of her father's upper-echelon employees, or one of her parents' many wealthy acquaintances who had been invited in the expectation that they would make a generous donation at the end of the evening?

'Penelope?'

Her father's slightly gruff voice broke into her musings and she turned to face him, apprehension stiffening her shoulders when she realised that he'd deliberately engineered a quiet moment to speak to her.

'You know your mother likes getting involved in these things,' he began, his tone slightly dismissive of any occupation not involved with high finance. 'She's gone to a great deal of trouble to organise this do tonight, and I don't want you to do anything to spoil it for her. The last thing she needs is for you to go spreading it about that you work in that godawful place—'

'But it's *not* a—'

'Don't argue with me,' he snapped, his face darkening with temper before he pressed his lips tightly together as though fighting to hold back any further words until he had his tongue under better control.

Penny's heart sank.

She'd had such high hopes that this evening could be the start of a reconciliation between them, but if he—

'Give me your word,' he muttered fiercely as he glanced swiftly over his shoulder towards the nearest group of people. 'I want you to promise that just once in your life you'll stick to normal social conversations the way your mother does.'

She suddenly remembered Wilson's advice and sank her teeth into the tip of her tongue as she swiftly counted to five and condemned herself to an evening of meaningless social chit-chat.

'Of course,' she agreed quietly, concentrating on keeping her expression blank under her father's glare—only allowing herself to relax when he turned away from her and set off to join his coolly elegant wife.

Penny watched the two of them together and marvelled that their marriage worked so well.

Her mother was an aristocrat to her fingernails while her father's recent title, a gong awarded for services to industry, was only a veneer covering Gregor Morozov, son of a one-time Russian gardener. He'd even taken his wife's name on their marriage to make the transformation complete.

Penny sighed and pressed her own lips together before she set her shoulders and pinned a smile in place.

It was only one evening, she reminded herself with renewed determination as she requested a glass of tonic water from the waitress. If it helped to smooth over some of the cracks in her relationship with her parents it would all be worthwhile.

For the next half-hour she circulated, smiling and thanking people for attending, and wasn't certain whether she was disappointed or relieved when she realised that there was no sign of the impeccably dressed stranger.

For just a second she felt an echo of the twist of arousal which had speared through her when she'd recognised the heat in his ravenous gaze when he'd stared at her scantily clothed body, but then she remembered the disdain which had followed it and couldn't help shivering.

'Penelope, dear?'

The utterly well-bred, cut-glass accent drew her gaze across to her mother, and she realised that while her thoughts had been otherwise occupied everyone had begun to seat themselves at their tables.

All she had been able to glean from her swift glance at the seating arrangements was that she was at the top table, as befitted the daughter of Sir Gregory and Lady Charlotte Moss-Edwards, with the MERLIN representative seated between her mother and herself.

She'd settled herself in her own chair when there was a slight flurry behind her and a lean masculine hand pulled out the empty seat beside her.

'Welcome, Dr Campbell,' said her mother with a practised smile.

'Call me Dare, please. It's very good of you to invite me, Lady Charlotte. I'm only sorry to have kept you waiting,' apologised a deep voice, carrying the slight trace of a Scottish accent. 'That was a phone call from MERLIN headquarters with some updated information I wanted for my little talk later on.'

The sound of his voice seemed to stroke over her skin like silky velvet, drawing Penny's attention so that she glanced up over her shoulder and straight into a pair of newly familiar dark sapphire eyes with the longest, thickest lashes she'd ever seen on a man.

'You!' she breathed in horror as her heart sank towards her elegant high-heeled sandals.

Her breath caught in her throat as his gaze flickered over her bared shoulder and down towards her seat as if he was once again seeing the evidence of her lack of underwear, and she felt the prickle of sweat across her forehead and between her breasts as she waited for him to say something.

'This is our daughter, Penelope,' her mother said, apparently oblivious to the taut atmosphere hovering over the two of them. 'She was the one who actually brought MERLIN to our notice and, of course, once we knew about your organisation and all the work you do, we just had to have this fundraiser to help. . .'

As her mother's voice continued to monopolise their guest Penny was finally able to draw a breath in the knowledge that the moment of danger had passed. All she had to do now was quietly eat her meal and listen to Dr Campbell's brief presentation before she could make her excuses and escape.

Thankfully, the meal passed uneventfully as she kept her promise to her father and returned the good doctor's every conversational gambit with a suitably bland reply, relying heavily on platitudes and inanities to deflect his attention back towards her mother.

Unfortunately, with the lack of mental stimulation boredom began to set in and, coupled with a long day at work, it wasn't long before she began to have trouble stifling her yawns, eventually having to try to hide them behind her hand.

'Too many late nights?' he queried softly as he leant towards her, his words for her ears only. 'I promise to make my presentation as short as possible so that you can get back to bed.'

'You're too kind,' she replied through teeth gritted

into a smile. 'It has been rather a busy day, and there'll be another one tomorrow.'

Too late she remembered her promise to her father, and she surreptitiously crossed her fingers that he wouldn't ask what it was she did all day that was going to keep her so busy.

There was no way she would be able to tell him about her career without her mother hearing, and if her father found out that she had broken her word it would destroy any chance of repairing their relationship.

'Another hard day at the hairdresser's, or will it be shopping?' he asked with saccharine concern.

Penny didn't know whether to be relieved that he was so far off the mark or furious that he thought her such an empty-headed ninny, but before she could come up with a suitably cutting reply her father was on his feet and calling for attention as he introduced their special guest.

'Many of you are business people and you will know as well as I do that there's no such thing as a free meal,' he began jocularly. 'So when you accepted my wife's invitation to come here this evening you knew that I was going to be asking you to put your hands in your pockets for a good cause. . .'

Penny joined in the appreciative laughter, knowing that most of the people in the room had been to such affairs in years gone by.

Her mother was well known for following in her own mother's footsteps as a society hostess *par excellence* and a tireless worker for charitable causes, and her father enjoyed basking in the shared limelight.

'This evening,' he continued, 'I'd like to introduce Dr Campbell, who has taken leave of absence from his work in one of London's top hospitals to volunteer his expertise for MERLIN, so if you'd like to give him a warm welcome he'll tell you what it's all about.'

There was a polite round of applause as Sir Gregory sat down and it rekindled as Dr Campbell straightened and smiled at his audience.

'Good evening,' he began, apparently completely unconcerned that he was speaking to a roomful of strangers. 'Sir Gregory was right about there being no such thing as a free meal because now I'm going to start singing for my supper.'

As the laughter died away he continued.

'For those of you who don't know who or what MERLIN is, it stands for Medical Emergency Relief International and we are a British medical charity which provides emergency medical care in disaster zones worldwide. Our programmes are carefully targeted to provide high-quality medical care where it is needed most, and we can respond to a disaster anywhere in the world within seventy-two hours.'

In less than a minute he had captured their attention and their imaginations and Penny could have heard a pin drop as he went on to explain how rapid response teams would be dispatched to arrive during the critical first phase of disasters when local infrastructures were in total disarray and people were at their most vulnerable.

'It doesn't matter whether the disaster is something natural, like the flooding in the Yemen where we had to set up malaria and cholera projects and rehabilitation clinics, or man-made devastation, such as the war in Rwanda which mobilised half a million refugees. Our brief is that we specialise in relief and reconstruction, not long-term development.

'Once an emergency has been stabilised we hand

over to competent local or international organisations, and monitor events in case of future need.'

As he continued speaking Penny's attention was divided between their charismatic speaker and his enthralled audience as he told them of the team of volunteers who drove a convoy of trucks and Jeeps through the shattered streets of Grozny to bring emergency medical supplies.

'When they finally arrived they found that there were only three surgeons still operating there—in a makeshift operating theatre created in the cellar of a hospital where the only anaesthetist had suffered a mental breakdown. . .'

He also told them of the nurse who had worn the full chador to comply with strict Islamic law as she fought to set up women's clinics in Afghanistan where the infant mortality rate for under fives was one in four.

But it wasn't until he began to tell them about the disastrous epidemic of TB which was sweeping across Siberia since the break-up of the Soviet Union that her attention was riveted to his every word.

When she heard that in the Tomsk area alone there were three thousand people known to be affected and that the death rate was expected to be one in three, she was fired with a desire to offer her own expertise.

Until she'd left school she'd seldom had real cause to argue with her parents, but when it came to her choice of career she'd finally stood her ground.

Her parents had been disappointed that she hadn't wanted to go to her mother's old finishing school in Switzerland, unable to understand why she should want to do anything as demeaning as nursing when there was absolutely no need for her to go out to work at all.

Still, they'd been able to console themselves that

she would at least be able to work in one of the better private hospitals when she qualified.

The final straw had been when she'd broken the news that she had accepted a post in a hospital in the East End of London, specialising in the treatment of TB sufferers. *That* had been when her relationship with them had hit an all-time low.

The sound of applause broke into her thoughts and she realised that Dr Campbell's presentation had come to an end.

Penny glanced across at her mother and saw the pleased smile which meant that she was confident that the total raised tonight would be a credit to her, and was glad that the evening had been a success.

Now, if only she could find a couple of minutes to speak to her erstwhile dinner companion, without her parents overhearing, she might be able to find out what the likelihood was that MERLIN could use her in Siberia.

Perhaps, if she stayed just long enough for the beginning of the dancing, he would follow the usual custom and ask her to dance. . .

No sooner had the thought crossed her mind than the small orchestra at the other end of the room struck up with a discreet fanfare and her companion rose to his feet to offer his hand to her mother.

'With your husband's permission?' he asked courteously, and led the delighted woman across to start the dancing.

'Seems like a nice enough chap,' her father commented as he complacently watched the pair of them circle the floor, then threw her a sharp glance. 'Did he have much to say during dinner?'

Penny kept her wry smile to herself as she realised

that he was just trying to make certain that she'd kept her promise not to talk about her occupation.

If only she could rid him of the notion that nursing—and TB nursing in particular—was a demeaning occupation.

'Not a lot—he spent most of the time talking to Mother,' she confirmed, not bothering to let him know that she fully intended to break her promise as soon as she managed to get the man to herself. After all, the meal was over now and everyone would be far too busy dancing to listen in on their conversation.

Her foot tapped as she waited for him to return to the table, the rhythm determined by her impatience rather than the orchestra's efforts.

Several young men glanced in her direction but she barely noticed, her eyes fixed on a head of dark blond hair streaked with sun-bleached strands as he leant towards her mother to listen to what she was saying.

Finally he began to escort her back towards their table, their progress delayed by the numerous people who wanted a brief word before they handed over the familiar oblongs of paper which meant that they were giving him cheques.

It took all her concentration to keep her in her seat when her newly kindled enthusiasm meant that she wanted to leap to her feet and hurry across to meet him.

She longed to start plying him with questions, but she had to content herself with watching the self-confident way he held himself and the pleasant manner he had of listening attentively to what people were saying to him.

In spite of her initial embarrassment at coming face to face with him, she had been struck by her renewed awareness of his physical presence though it was obvious that there was more to him than a handsome face and a well-proportioned body.

She couldn't deny that the subtle mixture of soap, shampoo and male musk which had surrounded her throughout the meal had helped to foster her unwilling awareness of him as a man, but the last hour had made that attraction deepen as she'd begun to learn what sort of man he was.

At last he returned a triumphant Lady Charlotte to her beaming husband.

'Thank you so much for inviting me,' he said as he offered his hand to each of them.

'I'm sorry you can't stay any longer,' her mother said with a regretful smile, 'but you can rest assured that I'll let MERLIN have the rest of the donations as soon as I've collected them—no one's going to be allowed to go home until I've emptied their pockets!'

Penny's pride was stung that he was apparently intending to leave without asking her to dance, and before she realised what she was going to do she was on her feet, her chair blocking his exit as she tried to disentangle her high heels from the hem of her dress without falling over.

'Allow me.' His deep voice was almost mocking as he slid one arm around her to support her while she regained her footing.

'Thank you,' she said breathlessly as she gazed up at him, her brain short-circulated by the warmth of his arm across her naked shoulder and his hand tucked into the curve of her waist. 'I was hoping that you were going to ask me to dance so that I could have a chance to talk to you before you left.'

'I'm sure you were,' he agreed as he released her, his hand smoothing surreptitiously down over her hip before he straightened and stepped back just far enough to break all contact between them. 'Unfortunately for you, I'm too streetwise to be attracted to people who have to resort to juvenile tricks like leaving their underwear off to catch a partner. . .'

Polly wasn't quick enough to stifle her gasp of outrage, but she was totally unable to make her tongue work as her brain seethed with words to refute his accusation.

'You've been luckier than most to be born into wealth,' he continued, obviously taking her astounded silence for an admission of guilt, 'but all your luxurious upbringing seems to have done for you is make you so bored that you have to get your kicks in this cheap way.' His eyes flickered down over her body in a graphic reminder of her scanty dress, their expression searing her like lasers.

'Hasn't anyone ever warned you what sort of danger you could get yourself into?' he muttered harshly, obviously having difficulty keeping his voice low enough so that his words couldn't be overheard by her parents or the other nearby guests.

'Haven't you ever thought that it might be a good idea if you got yourself up off your back and used your brain instead? Perhaps you could actually do something worthwhile with your life.'

CHAPTER TWO

PENNY'S anger was still simmering inside her when she decided to contact MERLIN the next day.

If she could have found some way of making an official complaint about their representative's rudeness without looking like a complete idiot she would have done so, but how could she explain that it was the fact that she'd gone out for the evening without her panties on which had caused Dr Dare Campbell to leap to conclusions?

As it was, once she made contact with the relevant person in the office in London, her enquiries were attended to with the utmost courtesy and she came off the phone feeling a pleasant glow of anticipation.

After the initial preliminaries she was swiftly invited to attend an interview, and had managed to arrange the date and time to coincide with her off-duty hours.

In spite of the fact that she was a member of a closely knit team, she didn't yet know whether she would be acceptable for MERLIN's requirements so at first she'd kept her plans to herself—she was half-afraid she would jinx herself if she started talking about it.

Once she knew that she *had* been accepted and placed on MERLIN's register, ready for selection, it was time to talk to her superiors.

'Are you handing in your resignation, then?' Senior Sister Hammid asked in surprise when Penny told her of her plans, the perfect crescents of her eyebrows shooting up towards her midnight-dark hair. 'Are you sure you've thought about this carefully enough, Penny? Have you thought about the effect on your career? Anyway, I thought you were happy working with us.'

'I am, Sister,' Penny assured her honestly. 'Very happy—that's why I'm hoping you'll help me to persuade the hospital to release me from my job as if I were doing a special sort of Voluntary Service Overseas.'

'I don't know if that would be possible, Penny,' Sunila warned. 'You couldn't expect them to keep your job open for you or the team would be short-handed the whole time you were away, and you can imagine how difficult it might be for them to guarantee to find you a similar post with the same general work pattern and an equivalent salary to what you're receiving now.'

'I know it seems as if I want the moon handed to me on a plate, but they'll be gaining too,' Penny pointed out.

'Apart from broadening *your* horizons with trips to foreign countries, what are the benefits you think they would be interested in?' her superior challenged.

'Well, for a start I'd be developing my management capacity under stress. As a member of a small specialised team, I'd be closely involved in leadership and decision-making which would mean I would grow in confidence and learn to exercise responsibility— apparently there is even the possibility that my time spent abroad with MERLIN would count as part of my continuing educational requirement.'

'In other words, you think it will be well worth my while to recommend that you're released and then to agitate for you to come back here when you've finished your stint?'

'In an ideal world, that's *exactly* what I'd like,' Penny agreed. 'Especially as it's my specialisation in TB nursing which has made me so welcome on MERLIN's register at the moment.'

'It's not as if there are too many of us,' her superior agreed.

'Exactly,' Penny leapt on her point. 'In England we've been horrified by this new TB epidemic—it seemed to come from nowhere when everyone thought it was virtually eradicated here.'

Sister Hammid was nodding as Penny continued, 'We hadn't anticipated what effect HIV and the increasing problem with drugs was going to have on people's resistance to the disease or the growing incidence of drug-resistant strains. But the scale of the problem in Russia is mind-boggling.'

'What sort of figures are you talking about?' Sister Hammid asked, clearly becoming involved the more Penny said.

'You mean, apart from the fact that Russia is over one hundred and seventy times the size of England, with more than five times the population?' Penny supplied with a smile which grew wider when she saw the effect on her superior's expression.

'In the Tomsk area alone there are three thousand people who have been diagnosed as infected with TB—and those are the ones they *know* about. The expected death rate is thirty per cent.'

'As opposed to the less than five per cent we can achieve,' Sunila broke in.

'Exactly,' Penny agreed. 'And it's not just the numbers involved. Everything's been made so much worse because of the vast distances and the problems connected with the collapse of the communist regime.'

'Politics,' sniffed Sister Hammid in a resigned tone

of voice. 'In the end I think most of the problems in the world come down to politics and politicians— local, national or international. . .'

It was several days before Penny heard that Sister Hammid had personally contacted the English National Board for Nursing, Midwifery and Health Visiting, who had been only too willing to beat the drum on her junior's behalf.

They were able to supply the hospital with up-to-date details of the many areas of the country which had already pledged their support for employees who wanted to spend time working in another country.

From time to time Sunila Hammid would give her the latest update on the progress of her application, and Penny sometimes found her thoughts wandering towards the man whose talk had sparked the whole idea off in her.

While she was still angry that Dare Campbell should have leapt to such an unflattering assessment of her character and condemned her, without taking the time to check his facts, she couldn't help remembering his lean good looks.

Nor could she forget the strange elemental awareness she had felt deep inside when he'd looked at her with heat in his eyes, and one small voice at the back of her head mourned the fact that she'd never have the chance to see where that awareness could have taken them.

Idly she wondered whether he had now finished his stint in whatever trouble spot he'd been assigned to and had gone back to work in London, but there was no way she would ever ask.

Penny grinned at the thought.

She could just imagine his reaction if someone from

MERLIN's London office was to mention that she'd been enquiring after him—he'd probably be terrified that the idle social butterfly with the sad lack of morals that he'd met at the fundraiser was out to track him down and get her hooks into him. . .

When the hospital's approval of her leave of absence finally arrived in a formal letter she was delighted, and it seemed like a dreadful anticlimax when, after that brief spell of excitement and uncertainty, life continued in the same routine.

She'd offered herself to MERLIN as a volunteer and had been accepted, and she'd established her right to an equivalent job to her present one when she returned from abroad.

Now she just had to go about her daily duties while she waited for some area of the world to need her services, caring for each newly diagnosed patient who came into isolation for barrier-nursing until they were no longer infective and supervising her other patients through the tedious six months of chemotherapy which would ultimately save their lives.

In the event, it was barely a fortnight before she heard from MERLIN again.

'Is that Penelope Moss-Edwards?' enquired a voice on the other end of the phone when she answered a summons to Sister's office to take a call.

'Speaking.'

'Our TB nurse in the new treatment centre in Nevansk, in central Russia, has broken her leg. What are the chances that you could be ready to travel out in three days?'

'Three days?' Penny gulped, her heart suddenly pounding with a mixture of shock and excitement.

She'd been looking forward to this day, but hadn't expected anything to happen this suddenly.

'There's a Royal Air Force flight going out with another delivery of medical supplies, and it would avoid spending money on a commercial flight,' the voice explained succinctly. 'Initially, it's for a six-month stint. Can you do it?'

'I think so, but can you give me half an hour to make certain?' Penny demanded as her adrenaline kicked her thought processes into top gear.

'I'll be generous and give you an hour,' the woman said with a laugh. 'Good luck—I've got my fingers crossed for you, and for us!'

Penny put the phone down and straightened, her head spinning with all the things she would need to do if she was to be able to leave for Russia in three days.

'Not bad news, I hope,' said Sister Hammid, and Penny whirled to face her, so lost in her own thoughts that she hadn't heard her enter the room.

'Yes and no,' she joked, still more than a little shell-shocked by how suddenly everything was happening. 'That was MERLIN. Their volunteer TB nurse has broken her leg, and they wanted to know if I could be ready to fly to Russia in three days and stay for six months.'

'Three days! Dear Lord, they certainly don't believe in giving you much notice,' she commented with a grimace. 'When do they need an answer?'

'In an hour,' Penny said as she pulled a wry face of her own. 'We've got one new patient being barrier-nursed in the negative air-flow room and two in the isolation wards, apart from a full list of clinics, and I haven't even been to visit my parents to tell them that I've volunteered to go with MERLIN yet.'

Sister Hammid's eyebrows shot up so high they nearly disappeared into her hair.

'Well, my dear, we'll cope with the work here, but I suggest you plan on remedying the situation with your parents *before* you actually leave the country.'

She glanced at the watch pinned to the front of her dark blue uniform and reached for the phone. 'In the meantime, I'll start the official ball rolling to get you released from duty straight away—you're going to need every moment if you're going to be ready in time.'

With her superior's easy acceptance of the situation, part of the problem was as good as solved.

Now all she had to do was find a good time and place to tell her parents what was happening, and that wasn't going to be nearly so easy.

'Good God, girl! Whatever's got into you now?' Sir Gregory raged before Penny could even finish speaking. 'As if it wasn't bad enough for your mother and me to have to gloss over what you're doing on a day-to-day basis *now* we're going to have to tell our friends that you've taken off to the other side of the world to mop up after shiftless Russian peasants!'

One, two, three, four, five, Penny chanted silently as she bit down hard on her tongue in an effort to control the anger flooding through her, but the implied slur on her beloved grandmother was too much to bear.

'Oh, I don't know,' she interrupted with icy precision, her voice clear and cold in spite of her outrage. 'Some of those Russian peasants aren't so shiftless— they even manage to marry their way into the upper crust of English society and hide their identity by changing their name—'

'Penelope!' her mother gasped, and for just a

second, when she saw the anguish on her mother's face, Penny regretted being so blunt.

'I'm sorry, Mummy,' she said, ignoring her father's roar of anger as she reverted to the form of address she'd given up years ago. 'I know you love him and you're incredibly loyal, whatever he does. . .'

'What do you mean?' her father blustered, his face darkly suffused with colour, but Penny ignored the interruption to continue speaking.

'I've always thought it was insufferably arrogant of him to pretend that just because he chose to change his name it changed who he is and where he came from. His parents were Russian peasants, and were proud of it till the day they died.'

'They'd never achieved anything by the time they died either,' her father shot back.

'No, they didn't achieve much if you count your achievements by the number of noughts at the end of your bank balance,' Penny agreed heatedly as she relished the powerful feeling of finally letting her father know the thoughts and feelings she'd been repressing for years.

'But,' she continued, 'if you count having the courage and determination to walk over a thousand miles with nothing but the clothes on your back while caring for a tiny baby, and then settling in a strange country where you didn't even understand the language, and if you count a life where you always gave an honest day's labour for your pay and always paid your debts, and if you count the legacy of love you left behind for the following generations then I'd count my grandparents the richest and most successful of people.'

'*That's* not success,' her father began, but Penny wasn't in the mood to listen to his version again and turned her back on him.

'Mother, I just called in to tell you where I'll be for the next six months,' she said, totally ignoring her father's voice. 'If you need to get in contact with me the staff in the London office will know how.'

She handed her mother the piece of paper she'd prepared before she'd climbed out of her car, the address and telephone number of MERLIN's office clearly printed in the hope that one of her parents might want to write to her at some stage in the next six months.

'Do you know what you'll be doing over there?' her mother asked with an unaccustomed trace of hesitance in her voice. 'Will you be working in a special hospital?'

'I'm going to be joining a small team—a doctor, a microbiologist and a pharmacist. I don't know much about the place yet, but apparently we'll be working with our Russian opposite numbers in their version of our isolation hospital.'

Her father's apoplexy seemed to have subsided in the background, and as her mother had come over to sit beside her and was apparently genuinely interested Penny continued, aware that her enthusiasm was showing.

'Nevansk is the place they're sending me, and it's the first expansion from the primary centre in Tomsk. That's where they've been running a trial, comparing traditional Russian methods of treatment for TB with those recommended by the World Health Organisation.'

Her mother smiled briefly and reached up to stroke her cheek, and Penny felt the slight tremble in her fingers.

'You've always dreamed of going to Russia,' she

murmured softly. 'I hope it's everything you want it to be.'

'It's all a stupid waste of time, if you ask me,' her father butted in, then paused to clear his throat noisily. 'But if that's what you're determined to do then I suppose there's nothing your mother and I can do to stop you—any more than we were able to stop you throwing away all your advantages to become a nurse.'

'Why would you *want* to stop me from doing what I've got my heart set on?' Penny asked simply as she met the dark brown eyes so similar to her own.

'You're as stubborn as your grandmother,' her father muttered in disgust. 'How many years did she live over here? All that time, and never once would she make an attempt to learn English. Now there's you, just as pig-headed as—'

When she heard what her father was saying Penny couldn't help laughing aloud.

'What's so funny?' he demanded with a scowl.

'You and Grandmother,' Penny chuckled. 'One of my earliest memories is of the two of you arguing— in Russian—about how important it was for her to learn English and how important she thought it was that you kept up your Russian.'

'Well, I certainly had to keep up my Russian to translate for her or she'd never have been able to cope with life over here, especially after your grandfather died.'

'Oh, Gregory!' This time her mother joined in the laughter. 'Your mother's English was wonderful.'

'What are you talking about?' he demanded irritably. 'She couldn't speak more than half a dozen words.'

'She always said that the only way she could get you to practise your Russian was if you didn't know any other way to argue with her,' Penny offered. 'She and Grandfather maintained that because you seemed to be determined to reject your ancestry the only way to make you practise was to keep her English a secret.'

'And you all kept it from me?' He looked stunned. 'How many years was that going on?'

'I only found out by accident when she started teaching Penny to speak Russian so it wasn't my secret to tell,' his wife explained gently. 'Anyway, she was quite right. You'd never have bothered keeping it up if it hadn't been for her stubbornness.'

The ornate clock on the mantelpiece began to chime, and Penny suddenly realised how much time had passed—time she couldn't afford to waste if she was going to be ready for the flight out.

'Look, I've got to go now,' she said as she reached for the jacket she'd folded over the arm of the settee when she'd come in.

'Oh, but I thought you might stay here for the night,' her mother said with real disappointment in her voice. 'You haven't even had a cup of tea.'

'Mother, I've still got so much to do to get ready, otherwise I'd love to stay,' Penny explained, for the first time in several years actually meaning the words. 'I've packed the clothes I'm taking with me, but I've still got to move the rest of my things out of my flat— I've found someone to sublet to for the time I'll be away so it won't be costing me anything, and a friend is storing the rest of my bits in her spare room.'

'You could have brought them here,' her father offered gruffly. 'The place is big enough, for heaven's sake.'

'I thought about it,' Penny said, 'but that would have meant a double journey in my little car or hiring a van, and there just isn't time. The other nurse out in Russia is in traction and isn't able to work at all so the team is already working short-handed, and there's a cargo of antibiotics ready for freighting out. . .'

Her mother seemed to hesitate a moment before she wrapped both arms around Penny's shoulders and enveloped her in a hug, scented with the hint of Chanel which had always been her signature.

'You will take care, won't you?' she murmured. 'It's such a very long way away.'

'Over three and a half thousand miles,' Penny agreed. 'But I'm getting almost door-to-door service, courtesy of the Royal Air Force who are airlifting a big delivery of antibiotics—some for Tomsk and the rest for our team at Nevansk—so I should be quite safe.'

'You'll keep in contact,' her father said, as he hovered beside the car she'd parked by the front door.

His words sounded more like an order than a request, but it wasn't worth quibbling when it looked as if some sort of truce was in operation at last.

'I'm taking my little camera with me so I hope to be able to send you pictures to show you what the area's like.' Her smile wobbled just a little bit. 'Knowing me, I'll probably manage to cut everybody's heads off, but at least you'll be able to see the scenery.'

'If you need anything to be sent out. . .' her mother suggested. 'Anything you've forgotten, or find you need when you get out there. . .'

'I'll get a message to you through the London office,' Penny promised, and when she saw the hint of tears in the eyes of her normally reserved mother she felt her own begin to prickle and reached hurriedly for the key to start the engine.

'I'll write as soon as I get there to let you know

how I'm settling in, but I've no idea how long the letter will take to reach you so don't worry. . .'

She watched the two of them, receding, in the rear-view mirror as she drove away, and when she saw her father wrap an arm around her mother, as though comforting her, she had to bite her lip and force herself to concentrate on steering the car to stop the tears brimming over and blinding her.

'Why did it have to take my departure for a hospital halfway around the world before we finally started behaving like a normal family?' she demanded aloud in the close confines of the car, and she could hear in the reedy tone of her voice the tremble caused by her overloaded emotions.

Penny was even more shell-shocked by the time the heavily laden RAF plane was ready to take off from its base not far from London.

She tugged the strap to tighten the belt across her lap, as if it would help her to ground herself in reality, while she listened to the engines roar as they were tested.

The fuselage shuddered as the brakes were released and then the power forced her back in her seat as they raced forward and up into the sky.

'Next stop, Sheremetevo Airport, Moscow,' she whispered as she loosened her white-knuckled grip on the armrests and ventured a glance out of the window for her last look at England for the next six months.

The first flush of green was almost bright enough to hurt the eyes as spring finally vanquished winter, the daffodils and narcissi already giving way to tulips.

It wouldn't be like this in Russia.

Moscow might be the same distance from the equator as Aberdeen, but the fact that it was surrounded by land meant it took a great deal longer to warm up from the minus twenty degrees it regularly reached in winter.

She shivered in anticipation and wondered if she'd packed enough warm clothing.

'If not, I'll just have to hurry up and knit myself a jumper,' she murmured as she thought about the patterns and wool she'd squashed into one case.

She'd been warned by MERLIN's office staff that one of the biggest problems for the team was finding enough to do in the long evenings, and she had tried to think of a variety of things to do to occupy her hands and mind.

Hopefully, the rest of the team would be welcoming, and she could spend much of her free time with them.

Several times during the frantic activity of the last three days she'd found her hands growing idle as she worried about her reception when she reached the other end, wondering how she was going to fit in with the rest of the team.

They had already had several weeks to settle the dynamics of the group amongst themselves, and she could only hope that she could fit in as well as their injured member had. It would be terrible if there was any sort of personality clash within the team—that could easily turn the next six months into a nightmare.

She gave a deep sigh and shelved that worry until later.

No point in borrowing trouble, she advised herself as she smiled up at the crew member who was coming towards her with a steaming cup. It was one and half thousand miles to Moscow, and then another two thousand before she finally reached Nevansk. She would meet them all soon enough.

CHAPTER THREE

'WHAT the hell are *you* doing here?' growled an angry voice just as she bent forward to reach for her luggage.

The biting wind whipped several long blonde strands of hair into her face as Penny dropped her bags with a clatter and swung round in utter disbelief towards the man whose cutting words still seared her dreams.

'*You*!' she exclaimed in horror as she looked up into the deep sapphire blue of Dare Campbell's furious gaze, abandoning the hope that he was just some figment of her overtired brain.

'You know damn well it's me,' he snapped. 'Why else would you have bothered travelling all this way?'

His hands were clenched tightly into fists at his jeans-clad thighs as he glared down at her, and she had the fleeting thought that he would have preferred to have them wrapped around her throat instead.

'Well, you've wasted your time chasing after me,' he continued before she had time to marshal her thoughts. 'I've got no time in my life for empty-headed debutantes with no morals and no ambition, so you can just turn around and go straight back to England.'

'Can't,' she retorted shortly, spitting the single word out through gritted teeth. If she'd needed a reminder of why she'd loathed this narrow-minded man from the first time they'd spoken, he'd just given it to her.

'Why not?' he demanded impatiently, already looking over her shoulder towards the precious cargo, being unloaded behind her.

'No transport, for a start,' she pointed out. 'It was strictly a one-way ticket.'

'Well, I'm sure if you smile at them sweetly enough those nice young men from the Air Force will be only too pleased to. . .accommodate you.'

'I'm sure they would,' she agreed in a saccharine tone. 'They've been courtesy itself ever since we left England—unlike the reception here.'

'There's no time to waste on party manners when there are members of staff to meet and consignments of drugs to transport,' he said sarcastically. 'In case you've forgotten what I explained at your parents' fundraiser, there's a TB epidemic raging right across this region, and *we're* here to do a job.'

'Well, what a coincidence,' Penny said as she beamed up at him with the broadest, most insincere smile she could manage, making sure she showed all her teeth before she added, 'So am I.'

'So are you. . .what?' he said with a dark frown, partly distracted by what was going on behind her and obviously waiting for his new member of staff to emerge.

'I'm here to do a job,' Penny elaborated with laboured patience, subduing a shudder as the chill penetrated her thickly padded jacket, and added with a touch of wickedness, 'Wasn't that what you advised me to do—get off my back and do something with my life?'

She was gratified to see the brief wash of colour enter his face when she repeated his crude advice, but he quickly looked away towards the plane again, glancing briefly at his watch as though concerned over the delay.

'Well. . .good. I'm glad you found something to do,

but I'm afraid I haven't got time to stand talking. I've come here to meet—'

'Aren't you going to ask me about my new job?' she interrupted brightly, earning herself another scowl.

'If you want to tell me,' he said grudgingly with another glance at his watch. 'Only I'm due to meet our replacement TB nurse and escort her—and the delivery of supplies—back to the hospital, and there isn't really time for renewing fleeting acquaintances.'

'In which case, let me save you some time by making the official introduction,' Penny suggested, holding out her warmly gloved hand in the best finishing-school manner and hoping her smugness wasn't too obvious. 'Dr Campbell, my name is Penny Edwards and I'm your new TB nurse.'

A deathly silence fell between the two of them, broken only by the banter among the group, unloading the crates and boxes of supplies and stacking them swiftly inside the vehicles with MERLIN's logo emblazoned on the sides.

'*You're* the new nurse?' he said incredulously as he glanced from her proffered hand to her face. 'How on earth did someone like you manage to pull the wool over MERLIN's eyes?'

Penny drew in a sharp breath of the frigid air and found herself silently chanting, *One*, *two*, *three*, as she tamped her anger down, reaching clumsily for the papers in her shoulder-bag without taking her gloves off.

'I didn't need to pull the wool over *anyone's* eyes,' she said through tight lips as she handed the wretched man the relevant documents. 'I gained my nursing qualifications straight from school, and after several years in general nursing I specialised. The last eighteen

months I've been working as a TB nurse in the East
End of London.'

Her chin was raised to a combative level and anger
was warming her cheeks in spite of the cold as she
watched the careful way he examined her paperwork—almost as if he expected to discover that they
were forgeries.

The gall of the man! she fumed.

Did he have such a high opinion of himself that he
expected every woman he met to go chasing around
the world after him? If the tongue-lashing he'd treated
her to was any indication of the way he treated
his girlfriends he must have very strange taste in
women. . .

'Right,' he grunted as he handed the documentation
back without a word of apology, 'they've finished
loading the trucks so we'd better be on our way.' He
turned on his heel and strode towards the air crew.

He glanced back when he heard the sound of her
feet, following him, and glowered in her direction but
she continued unabashed.

'All settled?' queried the young copilot when she
joined them, leaving his superior to speak to the gran-
ite-faced doctor.

'Yes, thanks, Geoff. In case you haven't guessed,
that's Dr Campbell who'll be supervising the transfer
of everything to the hospital. I'll be working with him
for the next six months.'

'Doesn't look as if he'll be a barrel of laughs,' Geoff
murmured wickedly.

His light-hearted humour was such a relief after the
tension of her exchange with Dare Campbell that
Penny found it hard to contain her answering laughter.

She was still trying to subdue a grin when the man
in question turned to face her, his expression so stony

that she felt certain that he must have heard young Geoff's comment.

She dragged her eyes away and stepped forward to offer her hand to the senior officer.

'I just wanted to say thank you for looking after me, Captain,' she said with a smile.

'It was a pleasure, Penny. I hope you have a productive six months. Perhaps we'll see you when the next delivery is due.'

Penny thought she heard Dare Campbell mutter something under his breath, but when she glanced towards him his eyes were fixed firmly on his watch.

'I hope you haven't forgotten that we're seven hours ahead of GMT,' he reminded her. 'You've come across another time zone since you left Tomsk, and we're getting short of daylight if we're going to get all these supplies safely unloaded and put away.'

Penny completed her farewells and followed his long-legged strides towards the small convoy of vehicles, then halted, suddenly remembering her luggage.

'Did someone find my cases?' she asked in a panic when she glanced all around and couldn't see them. She couldn't remember what had happened to them after she'd dropped them in her surprise at hearing his voice.

'They're in the back with the supplies,' he informed her in a long-suffering tone.

Reassured in spite of his exasperated attitude, she climbed up into the high cab and scooted along the bench seat, trying to leave plenty of room between the two of them when he joined her.

Their driver smiled at her and murmured a greeting as he turned the engine on.

'*Zdraste*,' Penny replied politely, enjoying his blink

of surprise with a mental thumbs-up for her grandmother's persistence in teaching her Russian.

For a moment she considered asking him about the
sights they were passing on their way towards the
hospital, but there was so much to see that her tired
brain balked at the prospect of concentrating on her
first conversation in Russian—on Russian soil—until
she'd had a good night's sleep.

The sight of the dingy piles of grey at the roadsides
and the wind-scoured, whitened fields had been a
graphic reminder that spring was still some time away
here. So while she was keen to know how long it might
be before she would be able to go on any sightseeing
expeditions she didn't quite feel up to asking yet.

Still, there was no rush, she reminded herself with
a glow of pleasure—she had the next six months to
brush up on the language, and a whole hospital full
of people to practise on.

For now, as the truck bounced over the ruts and
bumps of the tramlines bracketing the ancient cobbles
of the road, she had enough to do to stop her shoulder
colliding with the solid frame of the man who sat
silently beside her, his whole presence radiating disapproval and distrust.

Determinedly she concentrated on the buildings they
were passing, silently mourning the stark difference
between the grandiose ornamentation of the older
buildings as they sat uncomfortably beside the ugliness
of the slab-sided functional modern structures.

She would have loved to have shared her first
impressions with her companions, but suddenly the
weight of the many hours of travelling seemed to catch
up with her and she felt her eyelids begin to
grow heavy.

Penny valiantly tried to force them open, desperate

not to miss a single part of her first view of Nevansk and determined not to give in to the urge to rest them for just a few minutes, but it was no good.

The last thing she remembered before her brain shut down completely was an enveloping warmth and a deep rhythmic thumping which eased her journey into oblivion.

'Oh, bother. I'm all fingers and thumbs,' muttered Penny as she shoved another pin into her hair to try to subdue the slippery strands.

She was due to meet the rest of the team this morning, and wanted to make some sort of good impression—she certainly hadn't managed it last night. . .

She felt the heat of embarrassment travelling up her throat and into her cheeks when she remembered her arrival outside their accommodation.

The jerk of the truck's brakes as their driver had drawn up outside the small house which had been put at their disposal had barely penetrated her consciousness. It had been the deep voice murmuring her name so close to her ear which had drawn her eyes open so that she'd been staring up at Dare Campbell from close quarters.

Suddenly she'd realised that as she'd fallen asleep she must have slid sideways across the bench seat.

Whatever had happened, she'd ended up wrapped in his arms and cradled against his chest, gazing up into the shadowy depths of his dark blue eyes.

She couldn't bear remembering the way she'd almost fallen on the floor in her anxiety to get off his lap and out of the truck, her mumbled thanks less than gracious as she'd grabbed her luggage from the back of the vehicle and hurried in the direction of the room she'd been allocated.

Now she had the prospect of meeting him in a professional capacity to look forward to, and all she could hope was that the other two members of the team would be there so that she wouldn't have to spend any time alone with him.

She stepped back and took a quick look at the neat fit of her mid-blue uniform and tucked a couple of pens into the top pocket before she had to admit that she was only delaying the inevitable.

'Here she is,' called a voice with a distinctive northern accent as she reached the door of the compact kitchen. 'Perfect timing—breakfast's just been served!'

Penny followed the sound of the voice through into the connecting dining room and found that the owner of the voice wasn't much taller than she was.

His curly carroty hair was already beginning to recede, in spite of the fact that he seemed to be less than thirty years old, but his blue-grey eyes twinkled with good humour.

'I'm Simon Priest,' he said, holding out a welcoming hand for Penny to shake. 'I'm the microbiologist, and this distinguished gentleman is Maurice Stoneman, our pharmacist.'

Penny smiled at the tongue-in-cheek description of her new colleague. For all his professional-looking dark suit, the greying man who grinned back at her reminded her far more of an amiable cuddly teddy bear.

'And this lovely lady here is Lyudmila,' Maurice supplied, smiling in turn at the elderly woman standing on the other side of the table. 'She's the one who will single-handedly make certain that we all leave Russia at least two stones heavier than we arrived.'

Penny waited for the housekeeper to put down the plates she was carrying before she offered her hand and a murmured greeting, and was rewarded by a surprisingly sweet smile for her attempt at using the elderly woman's native tongue.

'Hey, do you speak some Russian?' Simon demanded just as she became aware that Dare Campbell had followed her into the room. 'When I first heard where MERLIN needed me I decided I was going to have a go at it but I got lost halfway through the alphabet!'

'I speak a bit,' Penny admitted, watching out of the corner of her eye as their silent companion arrived at one of the vacant seats at the table.

She didn't really know why she hadn't just told the other members of the team that she was fairly fluent in everyday Russian.

There was no reason why she shouldn't have told them that at one stage she'd been virtually bilingual— it had actually been a point in her favour when MERLIN had needed a rapid replacement for the injured member of the team.

Suddenly she realised how silly it was not to admit to her proficiency and was just looking for the words to explain her unexpected reticence when Dare broke the silence.

'It's not really necessary,' he said quietly as he pulled the chair out for her and left her to settle herself between Simon and Maurice as he sat down at his own place opposite her.

'Language isn't much of a problem,' he continued. 'The hospital has made certain that the staff working most closely with us are all reasonably fluent in English.'

He smiled his thanks at Lyudmila as she passed his breakfast across, and for the first time since she'd arrived in Russia Penny caught a glimpse of the charm he'd seemed to exude effortlessly with everyone except her.

'One of the junior doctors, Petr Ivanesevich, is particularly good,' Maurice pointed out between mouthfuls of wholesome, locally produced food, drawing her gaze away from the man opposite her to the food in front of her.

The meal was vaguely Scandinavian in style, with cold meats, boiled eggs and bread served with Russian tea.

'He was the Nevansk delegate who came over to London last year for the international TB conference,' Simon told her in an aside.

Penny listened attentively to the continuing conversation between the three men as she tried to eat her own breakfast.

Having worked in hospitals since she'd left school at eighteen, she was well used to eating at all times of day and under many different circumstances but strangely enough, with Dare Campbell sitting opposite her, her appetite was less than hearty.

Eventually she gave up the unequal struggle and contented herself by cradling her second refill of *chai*, the milkless tea glowing dark gold in the plain white cup as she drew comfort from the warmth.

Lyudmila soon came back to clear the plates away, leaving each of them with their tea when she disappeared into the kitchen.

In the distance Penny heard the sound of running water which told her that she wasn't going to find herself left with the washing-up, and was glad. All too often, the fact that she was the only female in a group of colleagues had made them assume that she would be 'mother' for them, and it was a battle she hadn't wanted to contemplate here.

'Would it be a good idea if we spent a few minutes bringing Penny up to speed before we go over to the hospital?' Simon suggested as he leant back in his chair.

'That's what I had intended,' Dare confirmed quietly. 'We've got a few minutes before we need to set off.'

'Well, the first thing we need to know is whether she is going to take on the leadership of the group,' Maurice said. 'Melissa was doing a great job before she broke her leg, and I don't see any reason why Penny can't fit her shoes admirably.'

'Actually, for the sake of continuity, I had wondered if it might be a good idea if *I* took it on,' Dare suggested.

When she heard the trace of steel in his voice Penny glanced up and found his eyes on her, their expression almost challenging, but before she could respond both Simon and Maurice began speaking at once.

'Good Lord, why?' Simon demanded.

'You can't do that, man,' Maurice objected. 'You're already fully committed in your role as team medical advisor.'

'Anyway,' Simon continued, 'this is the sort of situation where the nursing sister is admirably suited to being team leader. She'll be on the spot all day and totally up to date with everything that's going on, while you'll be backwards and forwards between the two sections and probably heavily involved with meetings and local hospital politics—if the last couple of weeks is any indication.'

'I take your point,' Dare conceded, 'but I still feel that it might be better if one of the original team members were to take on the mantle of leadership so that—'

'Just a minute,' Penny interrupted sharply, and all three of them stopped speaking.

'Don't you trust MERLIN's organisation?' she demanded as she glared directly at Dare, her chin up and her hands clenched tightly around her cup to disguise the tremor induced by her swiftly growing anger.

'Of course I do,' he replied immediately. 'They're damn good at what they do, and—'

'And so am I,' Penny broke in. 'I've been second in charge of my unit for just over a year and a half now, and the figures produced on World TB Day suggested that in the East End of London we were dealing with more cases of TB than the whole of Tanzania.'

'The situation in Siberia can hardly be compared with either of those,' Dare began, but Penny was ready for him.

'I already knew what the situation was in Russia before I volunteered my services, and I've been fully briefed on the specifics of the situation here in Nevansk. The least *you* can do is give me a chance to do the job I was sent here to do.'

There were several seconds of silence while Penny continued to glare at him, but Dare remained stubbornly impassive.

'She's got a point, you know,' Maurice said, obviously using his position as oldest of the group to act as peacemaker. 'Each member of the team has to pull their weight or the system won't work.'

'You've been taking up the slack since Melissa put

herself out of action,' Simon added, backing his colleague up. 'But if you insist on continuing you'll exhaust yourself, and ultimately you could jeopardise the organisation of the trial.'

The silence was longer this time, and Penny knew that Simon's contention had stopped Dare in his tracks.

He couldn't argue with the facts.

The whole reason for the team being in Nevansk in the first place was to introduce the World Health Organisation's DOTS programme for the treatment of TB.

The system of directly observed treatment, short-term, was new to this beleaguered part of Russia. The incidence of TB was rising so fast that it had already outstripped the money available to provide expensive and time-consuming traditional Russian methods of treatment.

MERLIN's initial test centre at Tomsk had gone a long way in just the first few months of operation to showing the worried Russian specialists that there was now a more modern and more effective method of treating their patients.

Even so, their small team was responsible for running the randomised trial at this second centre in Nevansk, and if the same level of expertise was maintained they, too, should be able to show that DOTS could halve treatment times, while also saving thousands of pounds per patient.

'It won't help our image if we are seen to be at odds with each other,' Maurice suggested quietly. 'We're already having to tread carefully because the Russian doctors are suspicious of our methods—they're rightfully proud of their medical traditions and are very bitter that the collapse of the old political system has left them short of funds, staff and medicines.'

'You've got a point, Maurice,' Dare admitted.

To Penny he sounded grudging but, rather than giving in to an outburst, she remembered to bite her tongue. She'd only reached a count of four when he spoke again.

'It'll take Penny a couple of days at least to find her way around and see her place in the way of things here so I'll keep a watching brief for her first week. After that, if everyone's happy with the way things are going, I'll hand over the reins completely.'

He looked straight at her as he finished speaking, and in the waiting silence their eyes meshed with the impact of two swords joining battle.

Part of Penny was angry that he was effectively putting her on probation, but when she made herself take a calm look at the situation from *his* perspective she was certain she would be able to see why he had suggested it.

'Sounds fair enough to me,' she said calmly. 'I'll need to pick your brain for the first few days, anyway, so you'll soon be able to tell me if I'm not keeping my end up on the job.'

She caught a fleeting glimpse of surprise on his face at her easy acceptance before he blinked and broke the connection between them, turning to speak to the other two.

'The new delivery of antibiotics has been stacked in the cold store, Maurice, but you'll need to check everything off against the cargo manifest before you start handing out prescriptions.'

'No problem,' the older man confirmed with a smile as he turned to explain progress so far to Penny. 'We've had to set up a central pharmacy but we're well on the way to the establishment of a foolproof pharmacy control system, and Petr is helping me to explain to the local staff how to initiate the stock card and requisition system.'

'As far as my side goes,' Simon added, 'I'm hoping you brought me a very early Christmas present in the form of diagnostic equipment and supplies. With the collapse of active case finding over the last couple of years, there's a huge backlog to get through.

'And with each test taking up to eight weeks before we get a result. . .' he grimaced '. . .I'm trying to get the equipment *and* the staff up to speed so that actively infected people don't have too long to infect others.'

'Oh, Lord!' Penny groaned and shot to her feet.

Simon's joking phrase about early Christmas presents had just jogged her memory. . .

'I'm so sorry, everyone,' she gabbled as she stumbled towards the door. 'I completely forgot all about them when I arrived. I'll go up and get them straight away.'

'Hang on. . . Forgot about what?' Maurice demanded, grabbing her arm as she passed his seat.

'They gave me a big bundle of post and parcels to deliver—it had all been accumulating in the London office—and I forgot all about delivering it,' she explained, feeling terribly guilty when they must all have been looking forward to news from home.

Suddenly she felt the renewed wash of heat over her face as she remembered *why* she'd forgotten about the mail entrusted to her care. All she'd been able to think about as she'd fallen into bed last night had been the way she'd woken up in the truck to find herself draped all over Dare's body.

She was determined not to look at him, but her eyes seemed to have a will of their own.

She had no way of knowing whether he was remembering, too, but her breath caught in her throat when she saw that his eyes were darker blue than ever, his gaze so magnetic that she was unable to look away.

'I'm afraid it'll have to wait until later,' Simon said regretfully, his light tenor voice cutting across the force field stretching between Dare and herself and releasing her to breathe again. 'It's almost time we were going across to the salt mines.'

'It won't take me a minute to fetch it,' Penny offered, her voice strangely breathless as her pulse continued to pound at the base of her throat.

'But it would take longer than that to open everything and read it,' Maurice pointed out. 'This evening will do—give us something to look forward to.'

His good-natured comment was the signal for the rest of them to stand up, all of them picking up their cups and delivering them to the kitchen with a word of appreciation for Lyudmila.

'*Spacibo*,' Penny murmured with a smile, far too conscious that Dare was following close behind her.

She wished that there were a few minutes for her to say more than one-word politenesses to the elderly Russian woman, but there obviously wasn't going to be time this morning—especially with Dare right on her heels.

As she made her way to her room to fetch her thickly padded jacket she had to stifle a sharp pang of regret that her grandmother hadn't lived long enough to know that Penny was finally visiting her Russian homeland.

It would have been wonderful to have fulfilled their long-ago dream together, but even if her grandmother hadn't been fit enough to travel Penny could have sent home letters and photos and maybe even tapes of her one-time compatriots' voices so that, even though she was unable to be in Russia herself, she could have shared in her granddaughter's journey of discovery.

'Penny!'

It could have been any one of the three men calling her, but the sharp twist of awareness inside her told Penny that her subconscious had recognised Dare's voice.

She drew in a sharp breath and found herself standing in the middle of her little room with her hands tightly clenched and her pulse performing crazy gymnastics.

'Stop it!' she hissed aloud, horrified that she was reacting as stupidly as some hormone-crazed teenager over the latest pop singer.

'Grow up,' she muttered as she drew on her gloves and grabbed her lightweight shoes, ready to change into when they reached the hospital building. 'Get your head together or you're going to end up chasing the poor man like Ian was chasing you.'

She pulled a face as she remembered the way she'd been bombarded with unwanted messages, invitations and gifts, and straightened her shoulders determinedly.

She might have met Alisdair Campbell weeks ago, but in spite of her reaction to his good looks she certainly hadn't struck up any sort of friendship with him—especially when he had accused her of being little better than some sort of high-class prostitute.

Their latest meeting hadn't fared much better, with his words blatant proof that his opinion of her hadn't changed much in the intervening time.

She remembered the scanty way she'd been dressed at the MERLIN fundraiser and had to admit that it hadn't all been his fault that he'd leapt to the wrong conclusions, and as she made her way to join the rest of the team she made a vow to herself.

Come what may, over the next six months, she

would *make* the man change his opinion of her. He was going to learn to value her as a professional, competent nurse, no matter what her hormones said.

CHAPTER FOUR

'*Zdraste*,' Penny said with a smile as she was introduced to yet another member of staff on her whistle-stop tour of the hospital.

She hadn't seen the building when she'd arrived last night and had been disappointed this morning to find that the facility was housed in one of the soulless, slab-sided buildings she'd seen on her way from the airport.

Still, at least it was more modern than some of the old rabbit-warrens of Victoriana she'd had to work in during her time as a nurse in England.

'This is Simon's domain,' Dare pointed out as she peered through the glass portholes in the lab doors.

Across the room she could see the young man's bright auburn hair as he leant towards a young woman seated at a brand new microscope.

She couldn't hear his words, but the way he kept glancing towards the young man talking beside him, and the way the young woman was nodding at intervals, told her that everything he was saying was being painstakingly translated.

It was obviously a time-consuming process, but she knew that once he had trained the first group of lab assistants to perform the essential diagnostic tests on the new equipment the rolling process would become faster and faster as each group helped to train the one following.

'If Simon has his way it won't take long before this microbiology department rivals anything in London for speed and accuracy,' Dare commented as they resumed the tour.

'He certainly seems utterly committed to passing on everything he can during his six months,' Penny said, impressed by Simon's complete commitment to his task. 'I half pity his poor translator, having to work at that pace for hours on end. His head must be spinning by the end of the day.'

'They certainly have to work hard for their pay,' Dare agreed sombrely. 'Some of the staff haven't been paid for several months because of bureaucratic hold-ups, and obviously it's had an effect on morale. But even with the problems of staff shortages and lack of supplies it doesn't seem to have had any effect on the dedication of the rest towards their patients.'

'With an attitude like that, just imagine what they could achieve if the DOTS programme was in place and properly funded,' she suggested. 'They could probably have the epidemic under control within three or four years.'

'In the meantime, we have to do what we can to demonstrate the efficacy of the programme, and trust to the urgency of the situation and the intelligence of the doctors to implement it as soon as possible,' Dare was saying as he pushed open the pharmacy door and called a greeting to the group of people working in the room.

Maurice only glanced up briefly to see who had come in before he raised one hand in acknowledgement and returned his concentration to the work at hand.

The pages of paper attached to the clipboard in his hand suggested that he was in the middle of checking off the manifest of the delivery which had arrived with her last night.

Knowing what his position was within the team, Penny could guess that everything was being meticulously entered into the new foolproof central pharmacy stock list.

It was the white-coated young man beside Maurice who straightened and smiled in their direction.

'I'll introduce you to Petr,' Dare offered as he let the door swing closed behind them and led the way across to the group of people clustered behind the small wall of boxes of drugs and other essential medical supplies which had accompanied her on the journey to Russia.

'You probably remember Maurice mentioning him earlier,' Dare continued. 'He's a junior doctor already on the staff here, and he's got a fairly fluent grasp of English, thanks to some time spent abroad with his Diplomatic Corps father. He's been an absolute godsend to us.'

As they approached Penny estimated that the man in question was perhaps an inch or two taller than Dare's six feet but he wasn't nearly as powerfully built, and his white-blond hair and grey eyes almost made him look like a washed-out version of Dare's far more striking colouring.

'*Zdraste*,' Petr said with a gleam of interest in his eyes and a wide welcoming smile as he held out his hand.

'*Zdraste*,' Penny responded. '*Kak dela*?'

She enjoyed seeing the way he blinked when she'd casually asked him the equivalent of 'How are things?', but she almost regretted it when he immediately continued speaking in Russian, firing delighted questions at her about where she'd learnt to speak his language and exclaiming about her fluency, all with the speed of machine-gun bullets.

For a moment she was afraid that she wasn't going to be able to understand what he was saying and, worried that she might just have made a monumental fool of herself, her stomach clenched into a tight knot.

Suddenly it was as if a switch clicked on inside her head and, apart from the odd unknown modern idiom, everything magically made sense.

'Wow!' exclaimed Maurice, his eyes going from one to the other like a spectator at a tennis match. 'I thought you said you only spoke a few words!'

Penny swung towards him, knowing her smile must be reaching from ear to ear so great was her delight.

'Actually, Maurice, I was being a bit cagey because I wasn't certain how much I'd still be able to understand,' she explained. 'It's some time since I've even heard Russian being spoken and I wasn't sure if I'd remembered enough to talk about the weather, never mind hold a conversation.'

'Well, take it from me, beautiful lady, you haven't forgotten anything,' Petr said gallantly as he reached for her hand again, this time bending over it to kiss the backs of her fingers. 'Let me introduce myself—*Doktor* Petr Ivanesevich, at your service.'

Through the euphoria of her rediscovered skill Penny became aware of an ominous silence beside her.

With an uncomfortable sinking sensation in the pit of her stomach, she turned to face Dare and found him glaring at her almost in accusation.

'It's time I showed you to your department,' he announced brusquely, barely allowing her to say good bye before he was striding out of the door and along the corridor.

Penny almost had to run to keep up with his long legs, but something told her that it would be the wrong time to ask him to slow down. Every step he took was evidence of a deeply simmering anger and she had no wish to make it boil over.

The room he took her to first had apparently been converted from one much larger space into six separate rooms, three on either side of a central corridor.

He didn't allow her time to do any more than peer into each small spartan room as he strode past—just long enough for her to see that all six beds were occupied.

'These rooms have been converted in the last month with the help of donations to MERLIN,' he announced, every clipped word sounding tightly controlled. 'Each room has ultraviolet light, and is equipped to provide negative air flow.'

Penny was impressed. Because of the cost of setting them up and running them, negative air-flow rooms were treated almost as an impossible luxury by hospital administrators, even in the more up-to-date TB units.

It seemed as if only those involved in combating TB on a day-to-day basis realised the importance of rooms specially constructed or converted so that air could only pass out of them through the window, via a particulate ventilator.

While she was taking careful note of everything Dare was pointing out to her, she was still conscious that he was angry with her. What she didn't know was why.

He could hardly be jealous of the way Petr had responded to her—the good-looking young doctor was obviously a well-practised flirt who couldn't help playing up to every woman in sight.

Besides, it was hardly her fault who decided to make eyes at her—it wasn't as if she'd done anything to encourage him.

In spite of her preoccupation with his volatile mood, she was delighted to discover just how well equipped her new domain was. Now patients coming in with their TB in a highly infectious state would be able to be nursed in complete isolation.

'I didn't hear any of the ventilators running as we went past. Does that mean that none of that group of patients is in the active stage of the disease?' she enquired, already starting to store essential information about her charges in her head.

'They've all got large families of young children so they're going to be here for the full two weeks to prevent any further exposure. After that they'll be able to continue their treatment outside the isolation unit— which means that they'll be able to go home to their families.'

'Is the unit full all the time?'

'It has been ever since the modifications were completed, but as the trial is being conducted on a random basis we don't have any say in which patients we're allocated or the severity of their condition—in spite of the fact that we believe our treatment gives them a better chance of full recovery, and have well-documented proof of it.'

'Hopefully, the results here will quickly duplicate those found at Tomsk,' she said fervently. 'Then there should be a good chance that the hospital powers that be will be persuaded to switch over from their traditional methods of treatment to DOTS.'

As he'd been giving her the guided tour he'd been pointing out the section which would be her responsibility, and told her briefly how they were trying to dovetail as much as possible with the existing regime.

They'd gone past a small treatment room and she'd observed one of the older nurses, supervising a patient taking his tablets and making the relevant notation on his record card. Then they turned a corner and encountered a waiting area with a small orderly queue of people, some with young children in tow, waiting to go through the same process.

Slowly, as she absorbed the sights and sounds surrounding her and took in the quietly confident aura around the small group of nurses working there, Penny's enthusiasm began to rise.

This was such a simple system to set up and run, but once it was working properly the effects would be very far-reaching.

She knew from her own work in England that the first stage for any new DOTS-based TB unit would be the treatment of the patients whose TB had been diagnosed as a result of their own recognition of their sickness.

Unfortunately, this was usually many months, or even years, down the road from the day when they'd initially been infected, and once the disease had taken hold every unguarded cough since then had carried the potential for infecting those closest to them—family, friends and workmates.

The thing she was really looking forward to was when they could start actively looking for people in the early stages of the disease—people who probably had no idea that they were sick or that they were already risking the health of the people around them.

While she'd been contemplating the possible course of the work she would be doing over the next six months, Dare had led her through to a small office with one wall lined with utilitarian filing cabinets.

He indicated that she should sit in one of the sparsely upholstered chairs, then perched one hip on the corner of the desk before he skewered her with eyes which had evidently lost none of their anger during the last half-hour.

'Earlier on this morning we had a discussion about the advisability of you taking over the leadership of this team,' he began in a quietly deadly voice which sent a shiver up her spine.

'Now, I don't know what your idea of leadership is,' he continued in a mock-conversational tone, 'but mine doesn't include being left in the dark about a new team member's strengths and weaknesses.'

The sharpness of his attack tempted Penny to strike back immediately, but one look at his expression as he drew breath to continue told her there was no point so she bit her tongue.

He was obviously going to finish what he wanted to say and probably wouldn't allow her to interrupt until he *had* finished.

'It would have been very much more helpful if you had actually told someone about your linguistic skills, rather than staging that little show to impress one of the local staff—a good-looking young man, apparently willing to be smitten by an equally good-looking nurse,' he added in a snide aside which scorched her cheeks.

'If you'd had some consideration for the fact that we are intruders as well as guests here and should cause as little disruption to, and drain on, the local resources as possible, perhaps you would have realised that it would have saved me dragging someone away from their own duties unnecessarily to act as your translator.'

An electric silence hummed between them as Penny bit her tongue again, deliberately allowing it to stretch for nearly half a minute while she counted slowly up to five, then all the way up to ten before she stood up to confront him face to face.

What she had to say would sound much better if he wasn't looming over her in the close confines of the small room.

'Have you finished?' she asked politely. 'Because, if so, I'd like to tell *you* a few home truths.'

She drew in a calming breath, conscious that her heart was beating an angry tattoo.

'To start with your last point,' she began decisively—only to be interrupted by a brisk knock on the door.

She stopped in mid-tirade and fumed silently when Dare held up an imperative staying hand. He glanced down at his watch and muttered an expletive.

'Come in,' he called impatiently.

There was a slight pause before the person outside the door reacted to the invitation and Penny wondered if she dared call out the Russian equivalent, but before she could make the decision the door opened.

'Excuse me, please, *Doktor*,' said the young woman in the doorway, her expression so apologetic that Penny had the feeling she must have heard that there was a difference of opinion going on in the room before she knocked.

'Yes, Yelena?' Dare said in a more even tone. Penny watched him make an attempt at a smile for the sake of the nervous-looking young nurse, but could see that his heart wasn't in it.

'I am reminding you that there is a meeting with the hospital director and the *Professor* in five minutes.'

'Thank you, Yelena. I'll go straight away, but first let me introduce you to Sister Edwards. She arrived from England last night.'

He glanced across at Penny as he beckoned the

smartly uniformed young woman in, his gaze very pointed as he added for her benefit, 'Yelena is one of the nurses seconded to our unit and she volunteered to be your interpreter.'

Before Penny could comment on his parting shot he was gone, pulling the door closed behind him so that all she could hear was the smart clip of his footsteps receding along the corridor.

'*Zdraste*,' Penny murmured distractedly as she inwardly cursed her lost opportunity. Dr High-and-Mighty Campbell needn't think that he was getting away with firing all sorts of accusations at her, without allowing her to clear her name.

Just wait until he finished with his meeting, she thought angrily. She'd be waiting for him, and he wouldn't find it so easy to escape a second time.

Meanwhile, her young colleague was standing nervously to one side of the door, wondering what on earth was the matter with her. . .

'*Prasteet*,' Penny said hurriedly. 'I beg your pardon, but. . .' She stopped.

What could she say without revealing how angry she was with the wretched man? That would hardly be professional.

'I understand, I think,' she said with a shy smile. 'It is the same in Russia, too. If he is a man *and* a *Doktor* sometimes he thinks he is *Bokh*—God?' she finished questioningly.

Penny couldn't help the wry chuckle which escaped her.

'As you say,' she replied in careful Russian, 'if they are men *and* doctors. . .!'

'But you speak Russian!' came the delighted exclamation, followed by a puzzled frown. 'But why do you ask for me to translate?'

Penny began her explanation in Russian, but soon found that her anger towards Dare had blocked the vocabulary she needed to continue and threw up her hands in exasperation before she resorted to English.

'*That* is why I need you,' she said in a resigned tone. 'My Russian was taught to me as a child by my grandmother, but I have no vocabulary for nursing.'

'But you will soon learn,' Yelena promised, reverting to slowly spoken Russian with a confident smile. 'I will teach you, and the other nurses will make sure you practise!'

'I don't know whether to thank you or to run away and hide,' Penny joked, suddenly certain that everything was going to work out well, then added impulsively, 'It is particularly special to me that *you* will be teaching me, Yelena, because you share my grandmother's name.'

Yelena exclaimed in pleasure and Penny noticed that the young woman also shared the same dark-eyed sense of mischief as her grandmother.

She deliberately tamped down the old anger which tried to surface when she remembered the way her father had tried to force his own mother to change her name to the Anglicised form, Helen, deeming it more acceptable in the social circles in which he now moved.

It was a testament to her grandmother's indomitable spirit that the thing she remembered most clearly was her father's fury each time his mother pretended not to hear him, only answering when he reverted to the name she'd had from birth.

'Now I must take you to introduce you to the rest of the staff,' the young Yelena announced. 'Then we will visit all the patients and it will be time to eat.'

Drawn from her memories, Penny cast a brief look

around the diminutive room, resigning herself to the thought that soon she would have to familiarise herself with the paperwork involved in the trial.

But for now she would do the thing she liked best— meet the staff and patients and start to form that all-important rapport with them.

The prospect of six months of ultimate responsibility for the paperwork would have been daunting if she didn't know that she would be spending just as much time with the patients.

Her time in Siberia with MERLIN was definitely going to be a hands-on operation.

As the two of them made their way around the compact unit Penny took the opportunity to question Yelena about the more traditional treatment being given to the patients allocated to the Russian medical team.

'What is the basic treatment of TB like here?' she asked while they waited to talk to the nurse who was supervising the next batch of patients taking their drugs.

'You mean, what was it like before the break-up of the Soviet Union?' Yelena corrected.

When Penny nodded the young woman's expression grew melancholy.

'There are many similarities between your NHS and our system—we both provide free medical treatment for all our citizens, with the addition of private clinics for those who want to pay for treatment.'

'Really?' Penny was surprised. She'd thought that everything was state-controlled.

'Before, we also used to have a big system to control and manage tuberculosis, with many people X-ray screening, long-time treatments, surgery and long times in hospital so the patients cannot pass the sickness to their families.'

'How long did the patients have to stay in hospital?' Penny asked as she realised that the organisation her young colleague was describing sounded very like the one which had existed several decades ago in England.

'*Dvahat*—nine?' Yelena paused to ask, and Penny nodded that the translation was correct.

'Nine months or one year,' she continued. 'Sometimes more. . .longer. But there was also money from the government, and accommodation and food coupons for the family of the patient. Now is all gone because there is no money to pay.'

'So this is why there has been an epidemic in Russia? Because the financial support for the patients has collapsed?'

'Exactly. And, while there is no money now to help the sick people and their families, there is also too little money for the hospital and for the staff so we have not enough people or medicines.'

'So you're saying that, unlike New York, where the epidemic is linked to AIDS, the epidemic in Russia has happened mostly because of poverty and poor nutrition?'

'And drinking,' Yelena added sadly. 'Many of our patients are. . .drunkers?'

'Alcoholics,' Penny corrected. 'But don't they realise that if they continue drinking while they're on chemotherapy they can damage their liver and kidneys?'

'If they cannot afford to give up their job to come into hospital they will die of TB, and if they come for treatment and continue to drink they will die of kidney failure. For some of them, as far as they can see they are going to die anyway so they may as well stay at work for as long as possible so they can support their family and their drinking habits until they become too ill.'

'But, that's so. . .so defeatist!' Penny exclaimed in horror.

'So is the thought of a thirty-per-cent death rate,' Yelena pointed out, 'so many of them seem to automatically think that they will be one of the thirty who will die and not one of the seventy who will survive.'

'In which case, one of our most important jobs when they come through *our* doors will be to tell them that WHO's chemotherapy regimen can change those figures for ever,' Penny declared fervently. 'In some programmes the cure rate is already well over ninety per cent.'

'If that is so we must make big drawings to put on the wall to tell them,' Yelena suggested. 'Pictures and words in strong colours that they will see every time they come to swallow drugs.'

'Posters!' Penny crowed in delight. 'Brilliant! And we can make them simple enough so that everyone can understand them—right down to the children so they can remind their parents how important it is to finish their course of treatment. Well done, Yelena. I'm so glad you're working on our team!'

The young woman blushed, but as the other nurse had just finished with the last of her current batch of patients she hurried in to make the introductions to escape her embarrassment.

'This is Olga,' Yelena began in English, obviously a little rattled by the compliment, then switched to Russian to complete the introduction. 'She didn't speak any English when MERLIN came here, but she has learnt some words from Melissa before she broke her leg.'

She turned to Olga, a slightly older and more senior nurse who looked more like the stereotype of the Russian shot-putter than the gymnast Yelena resembled, her dour expression a mixture of wariness and doubt.

'Olga, this is the new sister who came from England yesterday. Her name is. . .' She paused, turning towards Penny in confusion. 'What is the name we must call you?'

'My full name is very English-sounding—Penelope Moss-Edwards, but my friends call me Penny.'

'And what does this Penny mean?' asked Olga, pronouncing the new word carefully.

For a moment Penny was stumped. She'd never thought of her name having a meaning—at least, not in that way.

Suddenly inspiration struck.

'*Kopek*,' she suggested with a grin, then explained. 'A penny is the smallest coin in England, like the *kopek* is in Russia!'

They both laughed but decided to stick to her own name, and with just that bit of nonsense she seemed to have started to break through the older woman's reserve.

She'd been expecting to encounter it at some stage, having been warned that the effects of the political situation in Russia had created an atmosphere of frustration and bewilderment in the hospitals.

After many years of working in a system with standards they could justly be proud of, nursing staff now were no longer able to provide adequate care for their increasing numbers of patients, and they resented the fact. As far as Penny was concerned, it was only logical that they *would* feel that way. Not only must it seem as if they could never regain their former level of excellence, but now they were actually having to rely on outside help to control the killer epidemic which surrounded them.

'Now it is time to visit our patients,' Olga declared as she slotted away the last patient's record card and led the way out into the corridor.

Once again Penny marvelled at the speed with which MERLIN had been able to organise the conversion and equipping of the isolation rooms.

The whole unit was wonderful, containing the latest pressure filtration machinery to ensure that there could be no spread of contamination from any of the rooms.

Each patient existed in isolation from the others and the rest of the hospital population, visited only by staff trained to observe the strict rules of barrier-nursing.

'This costs so much, so much,' Olga said, shaking her head, half in wonder and half in despair, and gesturing as she locked away the containers of drugs.

Another cupboard contained the many boxes of sterile supplies for taking the intermittent blood samples necessary to check their patients' liver functions while they were undergoing chemotherapy. 'And all is a gift from people who do not know us.'

She seemed quite bewildered and disbelieving.

'From people who know how terrible this disease will be in Russia if nothing is done to stop it,' Penny pointed out.

'But you can treat so few, and there are so many. All have the right to equal treatment, but you choose. . .' She mimed a person making a selection, as if choosing from a tray of eggs or flowers in a garden.

'I know this sort of selection doesn't seem fair to the ones who aren't chosen,' Penny said, 'especially if they have been waiting a long time.'

One thing that Penny had found out about the Russian health system was that the idea that some patients should take priority over others was totally alien.

'But with TB,' she continued persuasively, 'first we must kill the disease in the people who are actively transmitting it to others—and we must kill it in a way that won't allow it to develop resistance to the drugs. *Then* we can treat the people who are carrying the dormant disease.'

'But this way there are so many drugs,' Olga exclaimed. 'So many every day for six months, maybe more. It is so expensive and we do not have the money.'

'But this way the patients only need to spend the first couple of weeks in hospital until they are no longer actively infective. Once we are sure that their livers are functioning properly on the chemotherapy then they can go home to their families. After they finish their courses of drugs they are cured of TB and the whole of their treatment is over.'

'But our old methods have worked well for many years. We have always looked after our people until now,' the older woman declared, the battle between her pride and her frustration and bewilderment clear in her voice.

'The world has changed, Olga,' Yelena pointed out gently. 'Russia is different now, and so are the illnesses and the treatments. The only thing that remains the same is that people get sick and need to be cured.'

'But the old ways—'

'What is wrong with using a new system if it cures people faster and cheaper?' Yelena challenged suddenly, as if she was becoming impatient with her colleague's continued harping back to the past. 'Is it just because it wasn't a *Russian* idea that you don't like it?'

Penny watched silently, knowing it was wiser to leave the argument to rage between her two Russian colleagues.

She thought Yelena had a point when she accused Olga of wanting to reject the DOTS system simply because it had originated outside Russia, but she wasn't going to say so.

Olga's mouth was pressed into a stubborn line as her intelligence fought with her emotions. It was several minutes before she nodded grudgingly.

'I suppose you are right,' she admitted. 'My father's cousin died of TB eighteen months ago. He was in hospital all alone for a year before he died and my aunt couldn't afford to take the family to visit him because there wasn't enough money coming in to pay for the journey. If he'd been treated this new way he could have been at home, yes? He could have been alive.'

'So, Olga,' Yelena said gently as she put a consoling arm around the older woman's slumped shoulders, 'we can't do anything to bring back your father's cousin, but we can try to save other people's cousins.'

Penny felt a burning pressure behind her eyes as tears threatened, her emotions coming close to the surface as she saw the sensitive way the younger nurse dealt with her colleague.

For a while, when she'd realised that Olga wasn't fully committed to the DOTS programme, she'd been worried that—in spite of her pride in her professionalism as a nurse—she might unwittingly jeopardise the ongoing random trial. Now she had no doubt that all would be well.

It seemed that her own arrival had acted as a catalyst to bring all the older woman's objections out into the open, where Yelena had helped her to see how illogical they were.

Now they realised that they'd spent so much time with their discussion that their ward round had to be brief, but Penny counted it time well spent.

The difference in Olga's attitude was already noticeable as she took charge of each patient's case notes and detailed their individual progress with more than a hint of proprietary pride.

The arrival of the patients' meals was the signal that it was time for Penny to go for her own meal.

After several hours of fierce concentration, while she'd tried to come to grips with a new medical situation in a largely foreign language, she suddenly realised that she was going to be seeing Dare Campbell in a few minutes.

The memory of their last meeting sprang to life, and the anger which had been forgotten all the while her mind was so busy flooded over her in a tidal wave.

Yelena was chatting happily as they walked towards the staff dining room together, but Penny was hardly aware of what she was saying.

Disjointed phrases were going round and round in her head as she remembered the sanctimonious way the wretched man had taken her to task, but worst of all was the way she had been denied the chance to tell him that, once again, he had leapt to incorrect conclusions.

She didn't yet know what a normal day's timetable was like in the hospital, but as the two of them left the cloakroom and turned towards the dining room her eyes were already searching for a head of sun-bleached old-gold hair, and she found herself vowing through gritted teeth that at some time today Dr Dare Campbell was going to hear a few home truths.

CHAPTER FIVE

'DARE'S still in a meeting with some sort of hospital board of governers,' Maurice told Penny when she and Yelena joined them at the table.

Penny's heart sank, but when she tried to work out why she couldn't tell whether it was because she wouldn't have a chance to set the record straight with Dare or because she wouldn't be seeing him. . .

Her eyes widened when she realised what she'd just admitted. Had she actually been looking forward to seeing the aggravating man?

Surely, it could only have been because she wanted to tell him how badly mistaken he had been about her from the very first time he'd caught sight of her.

She didn't have to close her eyes to conjure up the expression on his face when he'd realised how little she'd been wearing under her evening dress, nor did she have to delve very deeply to remember her reaction to the way he'd looked at her—the sharp twist of awareness when the darkening of his eyes had revealed his appreciation of her body, even when he'd disapproved of what he'd believed she did with that body. . .

Penny came out of her heated mental meanderings with a start, hoping that no one had noticed that her cheeks were on fire and her pulse was racing.

For a second, when she heard Simon talking about the anniversary of the October Revolution being celebrated in November, she couldn't follow what everyone was talking about.

'Also, some Orthodox Russians celebrate Christmas on the seventh of January,' Yelena told them as she elaborated on what was apparently a discussion of some of the oddities of Russian life.

'The mix-up is partly because Russia decided to adopt the same Gregorian calendar as England, and partly because Peter the Great decided to move the Orthodox New Year from September to January. It caused much trouble because the people said that the world couldn't have been created in January because apples are not ripe at that season, and consequently Eve could not have been tempted in the way described!'

Penny joined in the laughter, and managed to keep her mind on the general conversation for the rest of the meal—a delicious Stroganoff which reminded her almost painfully of the excitement of sharing her grandmother's forbidden forays into the kitchen.

Soon it was time to return to the unit.

As the optimum time for taking the tablets was first thing in the morning there wouldn't be many patients arriving to take their next dose of chemotherapy in the afternoon—usually just those who couldn't get to the hospital at any other time, due to transport difficulties or family circumstances.

Penny couldn't help thinking that if the numbers they'd been talking about over their meal were to be believed the volume was growing almost daily.

It was a good job that some of the patients currently attending the unit for their initial two months of high-dose treatment were nearing the end.

Hopefully, a proportion of them would be trust-worthy enough to be allowed to continue taking their drugs at home, supervised by another family member or even a responsible neighbour—otherwise the staff were soon going to run out of space and time to fit them all in when they needed to come three times a week for their continuing chemotherapy.

Still, she thought with pleasure, it was better that way than twiddling her thumbs with nothing to do while thousands of people were out there needing treatment. . .

She and Yelena were making their way back along the long stark corridor when her companion glanced over her shoulder, as if looking for eavesdroppers.

'I think some of our doctors do not like the new methods because they are frightened,' Yelena confided quietly, continuing one of the threads of the conversation in the dining room.

'Frightened?' Penny frowned as she tried to set her thoughts off onto a new track, and remembered that Simon had admitted to encountering some animosity from his opposite numbers in the hospital.

'Yes.' Yelena glanced around again and lowered her voice. 'They are afraid that they will lose authority. They have been very important for what they do in operating and treating these very sick people, and suddenly you are here, and your drugs make TB look like a very simple sickness which only needs a nurse to make better.'

'It's not quite as simple as that, but surely when they see how many more people can be treated in the same time and for so much less money. . .'

'Who knows how they will react?' Yelena said with an expressive shrug as they entered the unit. 'It should be the patients who matter most, but doctors have their pride and they are only human, after all.'

'In spite of what they would have us believe!' Penny joked, as she reached out automatically for a pair of gloves and expertly pulled them on.

There was already a small group of people waiting for them, and when Penny watched Yelena getting out the record cards she realised that they were all members of one extended family.

'The father became ill first. He thinks he caught it from someone at work who has died now,' Yelena told her. 'When his glands became swollen and he was coughing his doctor sent him here for X-rays and tests. When TB was diagnosed he was one of the first patients to be allocated for treatment on the DOTS programme.'

'And his family was diagnosed as a result of tracing his contacts?' Penny guessed.

'Well, they all live in the same building and eat together so they all had the chance to be infected.' Yelena smiled. 'Now they all come together, three times a week, for their drugs. That way, no one has a chance to forget. It is becoming almost like a social occasion.'

Penny could see what she meant as the banter flowed backwards and forwards between the various members of the family and the staff in the unit.

A quick look at their record cards confirmed that while the father had been diagnosed with active TB the other affected members of his family had not reached that stage by the time they were diagnosed.

For the father it had meant a disorientating two weeks in one of the isolation rooms, but for all of them now it was just a matter of conscientiously completing the six months' course of chemotherapy.

'Isoniazid, rifampicin and piridoxine,' Penny murmured as she marked the next card to cross-check against the drugs she was handing to a dark-eyed angel of a little girl. The three tablets were dispensed in a small disposable paper container, two of them white and the other a pretty shade of pink.

'Yelena, they do understand that it would be better if they could come for their tablets in the morning?' Penny asked, choosing to speak in English so that she didn't chance upsetting any of the family if they were having difficulties that she knew nothing about.

'Yes, but this is the only time that their son can drive them all here,' she confirmed. 'They *do* know that the tablets must be taken half an hour before taking any food.'

'And that it can stop contraceptive pills from working?' Penny prompted.

Yelena laughed and quickly translated the question for the family who also burst out laughing.

'My granddaughter is too young to get pregnant and my wife is too old,' quipped their patient, his sallow, leathery face creasing into a grin.

Immediately his well-upholstered wife reached out and thumped him.

'Too old?' she repeated indignantly. '*You're* the one who's too old.'

'No. No. It's only the sickness that made me too tired,' he declared, with a cheeky wink for his audience.

'In that case, old man, as soon as we are all well you can give me some more babies,' his wife suggested equally pertly, obviously intending to call his bluff.

'Oh, no! Not *more* babies!' he groaned theatrically. 'You will kill me just when I can look forward to a long life!'

They were all laughing as the family finally filed out, with a promise to return in two days for their next dose.

After they had gone there were just the last few late
arrivals to supervise and record before that part of
their job was finished for the day.

'Everyone has come,' Olga said with a satisfied
expression on her face when everything was locked
away. 'All of our patients have come every time for
the drugs, and if they do this to the end they will
be cured.'

'And if you encourage them the way you did today
they will certainly come to the end,' Penny said, giving
praise where it was due. 'You were right to remind
them that they must finish the course of antibiotics or
the TB will become drug-resistant and then we *cannot*
save their lives.'

Olga smiled, her face changing in an instant from
its usual dour expression to one of shy pleasure.

'It will become more difficult, I think, when they
are feeling well,' she said wisely. 'Then they will think
they do not need drugs any more.'

'*Then* we will have to be even more persuasive,'
Penny encouraged with a smile.

She didn't bother, at this stage, to mention that in
New York the number of patients who persistently
failed to take their tablets had forced the city to bring
in a law whereby those people could legally be locked
up until they were cured, and only then released.

Suddenly Penny noticed that Olga's eyes had
strayed to a point beyond her shoulder and, without
looking, she knew who had entered the room
behind her.

Suddenly her breath was frozen in her throat and
she couldn't face him, half-afraid of what she might
discover about the reason for her strange awareness
towards him.

'*Zdraste, Doktor,*' Olga murmured politely, and

quickly made her way out of the door, muttering something under her breath about tasks that needed doing.

Yelena shifted from one foot to the other, obviously uneasy with the strained atmosphere between her two English colleagues.

'You have some new patients for us, *Doktor*?' Penny heard her venture when the silence in the room seemed as if it would stretch on for ever.

Out of the corner of her eye she saw Yelena gesture towards Dare, and she couldn't put off the moment any longer, her chin lifting several notches as she turned to face him.

He was still wearing his white coat over his shirt-sleeves and had a bulky pile of files tucked under his arm, which looked in imminent danger of slipping, so she stepped aside so that he had access to the X-ray view-box.

She still hadn't managed to steel herself to meet his eyes, but when he stayed just inside the door, without taking advantage of the space she had made, she finally had to look up.

His dark blue eyes were searching her face, almost as if he was looking for something, and she felt a growing heat in her cheeks as she forced herself to stand still under his silent scrutiny.

'*Doktor*?' Yelena said hesitantly, obviously nonplussed by the electricity in the air.

He blinked and looked towards the pile of case files in his hand, as if he wasn't quite sure how they got there, then shook his head. Penny could almost hear the gears grinding as he switched his thoughts towards the mountain of work in his hands.

'Yes, Yelena,' he said in a distracted voice. 'The X-rays of the latest cases referred to our unit have just been developed so I brought them over here to examine.'

He deposited the pile of heavy manila envelopes on the narrow table under the view-box and flicked the switch to illuminate the flat white screen before he reached inside the top one for the first pair of plates.

'Hmm,' he grunted as he slipped the two of them up under the retaining clips and leaned forward to concentrate.

Suddenly he was every inch the professional, every trace of distraction banished as if it had never happened.

'Not good,' he muttered, and Penny had to drag her eyes away from their contemplation of his striking profile to look at the posterior—anterior chest film.

As soon as she looked at the area which displayed the region where the lungs were she could see why he'd muttered.

'It's secondary tuberculosis, isn't it?' she said when she saw the distinctive white markings.

The words might have sounded like a question, but after the last few years she had spent closely involved in the treatment of TB she had seen enough X-rays to distinguish most of the variations presenting at a specialist chest unit.

At first she used to confuse some cases of primary tuberculosis infection with pneumonia, but once she'd learned to look for the characteristic enlarged lymph nodes it had become easy.

This was another matter, the upper portions of both lungs showing the radiological evidence of cavitation, scarring and nodules typical of the secondary disease.

'Well, we won't need to wait weeks for his sputum culture tests to come back from the lab to make the diagnosis,' Dare said with a sigh.

'Well, at least that means we know to get him started on chemotherapy straight away. That could save another twenty people from being infected by him in the meantime.'

At his request, Penny acted as secretary, waiting while he made a notation on the accompanying file then sliding plates and notes back into the envelope while he started on the next one.

Over the next hour they worked their way steadily through each case, so at ease with each other in the clinical atmosphere that it was almost as if those electric moments of silent scrutiny had never happened.

In spite of her pleasure at their new working rapport, Penny grew more depressed as the time passed, but it wasn't because she resented the way he'd apparently been able to shut her out of his thoughts but because one set of X-rays after another showed clear evidence of tuberculosis.

'How are we ever going to deal with all of these?' she asked when she slapped the last big beige envelope down on top of the pile. 'We've only got the six beds for isolation and there must be nearly twenty new patients there, all of them obviously actively infectious. They need to be kept out of circulation.'

'Twenty-one,' he corrected wryly.

'It might as well be fifty-one—we still can't find enough beds for them all. The unit's too small.'

'That's why I was in a meeting with the hospital bigwigs for half the day,' he said in a tone of grim resignation as he linked his fingers behind his neck and stretched his elbows wide, as though all the muscles in his neck and shoulders were too tight.

'What. . .what did they have to say?' she asked, distracted for a moment by the glimpse of smooth brown skin at his waist when his shirt pulled partly out of the waistband of his trousers.

At her question Dare turned towards her, and the light from the X-ray view-box gleamed briefly on the pattern of dark gold hairs across the flat expanse of his belly before he dropped his arms and they were hidden again.

'I asked them if there was any way they could let me have some more beds for this little lot. . .' he nodded towards the pile '. . .always presuming that the results showed they were actively infected.'

'And?' she prompted.

'And they said they'll see what they can do. They're going to let me know in a couple of days.'

He scowled fiercely, drawing his brows together over the lean blade of his nose.

'Aren't you pleased?' Penny demanded, nonplussed by his apparently half-hearted response to the news.

'Unfortunately, they also very helpfully pointed out a rather inescapable problem—the fact that they haven't got enough staff for the patients they're treating now, and certainly wouldn't be able to release any of them to take care of another twenty-plus of mine.'

'But it's only for two weeks,' she exclaimed. 'Didn't you explain that at the end of the two weeks they'll be able to continue the treatment from home?'

'Of course I did, but they countered *that* argument with the probability that those people would immediately be replaced by even more diagnosed cases, and implied that if they gave in to me in this instance MERLIN could end up taking over the whole hospital!'

'I wish we could,' Penny said fervently. 'When Olga told me about some of the methods they were using when she started nursing twenty years ago I was too afraid of the answer to ask her if they're still doing things that way now.'

'Well, the whole thing could be academic if the powers that be turn the idea down,' he pointed out. 'And even if they agree to it I still wouldn't be able to staff it.'

'And, in the meantime, there are twenty-one people out there who've had active tuberculosis diagnosed, and who are continuing to put people around them at risk of infection because we can't start treating them because we haven't got enough beds.'

'Welcome to the real world—not a trace of glamour in sight,' he said tiredly as he tapped the files into a neat pile with a practised flick against the table. 'This is just the sort of situation that will have you scurrying back to your nice-and-easy existence among the rest of the upper-crust double-barrelled names in the commuter belt.'

Penny opened her mouth to fire a blistering salvo in rebuttal, but she remembered just in time that there were other people nearby and bit her tongue.

She had counted up to ten before she had any confidence that she wasn't going to scream at him, then drew in a deep breath.

'It's a shame it's not an Olympic event,' she began softly, mindful of their potential audience and forcing the words out with grim control from between clenched teeth. 'Because, Dr Campbell, I'm certain you'd win the gold medal—for jumping to conclusions!' She whirled away and left him illuminated by the forgotten X-ray view-box.

Penny was still fuming at the injustice of Dare's remark when she returned to their shared accommodation later that afternoon.

What right did he have to assume that she was only interested in an easy life? Hadn't the fact that she'd taken the trouble to volunteer to work for MERLIN proved that she wasn't after a glamorous existence?

What galled her most was that they'd spent quite a lot of time together since she'd arrived in Nevansk, especially this afternoon while he'd gone through the new patient files, and he still didn't seem to be able to look past their first disastrous meeting.

Whether by accident or design, she hadn't seen Dare since she'd stormed away from him, but that didn't mean that she'd been able to keep him out of her head, her thoughts veering between anger at his attitude towards her and appreciation of his diagnostic skills.

As she looked back on the events of the afternoon she couldn't believe that their apparent rapport could have been so short-lived.

She'd actually been thinking that jet lag must have caused her to exaggerate their confrontation when she'd arrived at the airport on the outskirts of Nevansk.

Well, his latest outburst of unprovoked ridicule and the implication that she lacked the determination to see the job through had certainly put paid to that idea.

It had also put paid to her half-formed intention to let his previous accusations die on their own.

'Not likely,' she muttered as she scooped up the three piles of letters and parcels and prepared to take them down to the others. 'This time he's going to get both barrels—between the eyes!'

Out in the corridor Maurice was leaning against the frame of Simon's door while they chatted, his cuddly teddy-bear frame looking eminently comfortable and relaxed in a pair of corduroy trousers and an Argyll sweater.

'Here, you two, grab hold of this lot,' she instructed

as she juggled the three piles, her cheerfulness fuelled by a sense of nervous anticipation mixed with dread. 'You should just have time to sort the bills out from the billets-doux by the time Lyudmila has the meal on the table.'

'Hey! This is great,' Simon said enthusiastically. 'I'd forgotten all about the post. Is the rest for Dare?'

'Yes. . . Do you know where he is?' She surreptitiously crossed her fingers that the wretched man had returned to their temporary home and was somewhere out of earshot of these two. If she got the chance to tell him what she thought of him she wanted to be able to do it without worrying that every word could be overheard by the rest of the team.

'He went down about five minutes ago,' Maurice informed her in a preoccupied voice as he started flicking through his pile of treasure trove. 'Should be in the sitting room with his feet up, if he knows what's good for him,' he mumbled as he wandered across the hall in the direction of his own room.

Penny breathed a small sigh of relief that Simon and Maurice were going to be occupied for the next few minutes at least, and set off for the stairs.

The last thing she wanted to do was disrupt the smooth working of the three original members of the team but, by the same token, she wouldn't be able to do her own job properly if she was going to be subjected to intermittent bouts of unwarranted character assassination.

For everyone's sake, she was going to have to clear the air, she told herself as she hovered outside the sitting-room door, and the only way to do that was to take the bull by the horns.

'This is your share of the post,' she announced as she forced herself to walk briskly across the room towards Dare. 'I've given Simon and Maurice theirs.'

Dare was sitting at one end of the long settee, his head angled back wearily into the corner and his feet reaching almost halfway across the small rug.

He, too, was dressed casually, his jeans worn enough to have become comfortable old friends, and his jumper looked like a complicated hand-knit.

As she approached with the small bundle in her outstretched hand he slid his feet out of her way and held out his own hand. His fingers were very warm when she accidentally touched them, and only her quick reflexes prevented her from dropping the whole lot in his lap.

'Thank you,' he said formally, as he immediately started to examine the top item. 'It's been three weeks since the last flight out so this lot must have been piling up in the corner of the office in London.'

Penny drew in a steadying breath, and before she could change her mind began speaking.

'Before you get involved with your post I need to have a word with you,' she said, then worried her lower lip with her teeth while she waited for his response.

It wasn't slow in coming.

His eyes rose to capture her gaze, and for some reason she had the feeling that he was making a point of hiding his thoughts from her.

'In connection with. . .?' he prompted flatly, his eyes so cold that suddenly her knees started to shake.

Was this a good idea, she wondered in a last-minute burst of panic, or would confronting him like this only make matters worse?

'I suppose that now you've seen what you're up against you want me to arrange for you to fly back home?' he accused suddenly, the barely disguised anger in his voice startling her. 'It didn't take you long to discover that a theatrical revelation that you possess some linguistic skills isn't enough for the long haul, did it?'

'But that's not why I—' she began, but he wasn't listening.

'Well, you're out of luck this time because I couldn't get you on a flight to England at such short notice, even if I wanted to, so you'll just have to roll up your sleeves and get on with it. You never know, finding out at first hand how the other half lives might actually do you some good.'

'You. . .you insufferable snob,' she hissed, as all her determination to keep calm disappeared in a puff of smoke. 'For your information, I have no intention of going back to England until I have finished the job I came here to do.'

Her pulse was a roaring sound in her ears and she was rhythmically clenching her fists as she fought to control the desire to thump him. . .hard.

'As for your repeated sneering at what you call my "linguistic skills", if you contact MERLIN's London office you'll find that I told them all about my doubtful proficiency in Russian when I first contacted them about volunteering. You'll probably find that the information is in one of those letters.' She gestured towards the bundle she'd just given him.

'And, just in case you think I'm holding anything back,' she continued, not giving him any chance to interrupt, 'I also speak slightly better than schoolgirl French and can say, "No, thank you," in at least five other languages.'

'That's hardly relevant to—' he began, but she cut him off as though he hadn't bothered.

'As for your accusation that I deliberately hid my

knowledge of Russian until I could make a show of it,' she ploughed on, 'I was taught to speak it as a child by my grandmother, who died six years ago aged eighty-two. I haven't spoken a word of it since—until today when, much to my delight, I found it all coming back to me.'

Whether it was the mention of her beloved grandmother on top of the stress of the last few days she didn't know, but suddenly she realised that she was close to tears and shaking too much to continue.

All she could think about was escaping up to the sanctuary of her room and shutting the door on this whole episode, and she whirled away from the laser-like intensity of his gaze to hurry towards the door.

'Penny?' he called before she'd taken her first step into the narrow hallway.

For a second she was tempted to ignore him but there was a strange tone in his voice—an uncharacteristic hint of uncertainty even in that single word, and she paused, waiting to see what he would say.

'I'm sorry,' he said simply, his voice soft and low.

'W-what?' She turned slowly, hardly able to believe what she'd heard.

'I said, "I'm sorry",' he repeated as he stared at the pile of letters clenched in one lean hand. Then his gaze flicked up to meet hers and she had the brief impression of pain and regret in their blue depths before the shutters came down again. 'I was completely out of line.'

'Yes, you were,' she agreed, finally able to meet his gaze fearlessly. 'You had no reason to speak to me like that.'

'Nor did I have the right,' he admitted candidly.

He hesitated for a moment and glanced away, his

jaw moving as if he was grinding his teeth together while he struggled with a problem.

Suddenly he stood up, taking no notice as the letters cascaded from his hand onto the floor as he strode swiftly towards the window. He pulled one curtain back and gazed blindly out into the gathering darkness.

She stood, watching and waiting, until finally his voice rasped over his shoulder into the silence between them.

'If I've made the situation here too uncomfortable for you to stay then you're at liberty to say so and I'll try to arrange transport as soon as I can.'

The quietly spoken words hit Penny like a blow.

She'd just been allowing herself to think that, in spite of the strange awareness between them, their differences had been resolved and they would be able to work together amicably. Now it almost seemed as if he didn't want her here any more.

'Do you want me to leave?' she demanded. She had to force the words out past the lump in her throat, but she needed to know.

'God, no!' he exclaimed fervently, whirling to face her. 'That's the last thing I want.'

Her spirits began to rise like a helium-filled balloon and she felt a smile begin to creep across her face.

'The team can't function without you,' he continued seriously. 'There were only a few days between Melissa's accident and your arrival, but trying to cope with the organisational side of her job as well as my own wasn't working.

'It was especially stressful, knowing that I didn't have time to supervise the local staff to make sure that they were following the chemotherapy protocol correctly.'

It took a conscious effort, but Penny managed to

pin her smile in position even while her spirits were
plunging as if they'd sprung a leak.

For one brief moment her heart had leapt when he'd
been so adamant that he didn't want her to leave,
believing that it was her as a person he wanted to stay.

No chance.

As he continued speaking he soon made it obvious
that his priorities lay solely with the diagnosis and
treatment of his patients, and she realised that the
sooner she returned to being the same level-headed
woman she'd been before she butted heads with the
exasperating man the better it would be.

At least their confrontation had achieved one
thing—he seemed to have changed his tune about her
usefulness to the team. Now he actually seemed to be
admitting that they couldn't function properly
without her.

'*Obed, Doktor*,' came a hesitant voice at the door,
and they turned simultaneously to stare at Lyudmila,
so startled by her intrusion into the scene that she
seemed almost to have come from another planet.

'Pardon?'

Dare was the first to recover, but obviously had no
idea what the poor woman was trying to say.

'She said the dinner's ready,' Penny translated. 'I'll
just go up and let the others know.' And before he
could say a word she had seized the opportunity for
a few seconds to herself and was out of the hall door
and hurrying up the stairs.

CHAPTER SIX

THE truce between Dare and herself had been slightly uncomfortable for the first day, but Penny had tried to make certain that she was far too busy to think of him.

Unfortunately, the unit was too small and their team had to work far too closely together to be able to keep that up for long.

It seemed that every time she turned around he was there, and even when he was occupied elsewhere the Russian staff were talking about him or about topics which led back to thoughts of him.

'I have been talking to my friends,' Olga announced a couple of days later. 'They worked here in the hospital with me, but when things became so bad with so many sick people and not much money for drugs and wages they did not work here any more.'

'Had you known them a long time?' Penny asked, fascinated by this rare glimpse into the life of this very private lady.

'Fifteen, twenty years,' she said, with a shrug that tried hard to be casual but failed. 'They were like sisters to me.'

Penny's heart went out to her when she heard the suppressed misery in her voice. She had already gathered that Olga had never married, and that when her mother had died a year ago she had been left alone in the world.

The information that the colleagues she had known for half her lifetime had also been, to all intents and purposes, taken away at the same time seemed to have contributed to the air of loneliness which often surrounded her.

'Were you telling them about the terrible English people, coming into your good Russian hospital and ordering you about?' Penny asked, then marvelled at the fact that in just a few days the relationship between herself and the previously suspicious woman could have built up to the stage where she could joke about such things.

'Of course,' Olga returned with a sparkle of humour in her eyes and one of her surprisingly sweet smiles. 'But I also made them jealous when I told them about the new way you are trying to cure our people of this terrible illness.'

'They're jealous?'

'Yes, because they were good nurses and enjoyed trying to make sick people well again. They miss their work.'

'That's a shame,' Penny said sympathetically. 'But if they weren't being paid regularly then they would have to find other jobs to help support their families.'

'But they have not taken other work because it is nursing they love,' Olga said. 'Lana has husband who has a good job and Valeria and Galina now have no children at home, but all have mother living with them.'

'Mother?' Penny questioned. The way Olga had said it there was obviously a special significance in the fact that a member of the older generation was living with each of her old colleagues.

'There is a saying in Russia, "If you haven't got a grandmother, buy one!" If you had lived in Russia you would know how important this is,' Olga said with a wry chuckle. 'It can take sometimes five hours a day to queue for food and such in the shops, and this is a job which the grandmothers can do while their daughters or sons are at work, earning the money.'

Suddenly Penny understood.

'So when your friends stay home they have nothing to do because they don't want to stop the grandmothers from feeling useful.'

'Exactly. And now they are so bored to be at home,' Olga said, and gave a small smile. 'They used to feel sorry for me that all I had was my work and my mother while they were so busy with their husbands and children. But now they *envy* me that at least I have my work to keep me busy.'

'It's even more of a shame when you know that the hospital needs their skills,' Penny commented, her thoughts returning to her conversation with Dare about the lack of staff to nurse the increasing numbers of confirmed tuberculosis cases.

'Well, it's time to get busy,' said Penny, snapping out of her introspection as she heard the sound of voices in the waiting area. 'The first lot of patients seems to have arrived early for their tablets.'

'I have the keys to the drugs cupboard,' Olga said briskly as she unhooked them from her belt, openly relishing the start of another day's work. 'Will you get the boxes of record cards out?'

Dare was late coming back to the house that afternoon, and the rest of the team were just wondering whether to start the evening meal without him when he arrived.

Penny couldn't stop her eyes from admiring the way his hair had been tousled by the gusty wind outside, or stop herself appreciating the way that same wind had whipped colour into his face along his cheekbones.

'Problems?' Maurice ventured when he saw the thunderous expression on Dare's face.

'It's the same old story,' he muttered angrily. 'As fast as you solve one problem there are another couple, waiting to take its place.'

'So, which are you going to tell us first—the good news or the bad?' asked Simon as he lay with his wiry body sprawled diagonally across more than half of the settee.

'Well, the good news is that the committee has decided that they'll make that long barracks of a ward available to us for that new batch of patients we X-rayed the other day.'

'And the bad news?' Maurice prompted, but Penny had a feeling she knew exactly what was coming.

'Let me guess,' she said. 'No nurses to staff it and no money to recruit more staff?'

'Right first time,' he said, adding a parody of a smile to his nod in her direction. 'And the fact that I've been anticipating exactly this outcome for days now, and have been racking my brains for a solution, doesn't mean that I've come up with anything.'

Lyudmila had obviously heard Dare come in because she stuck her head round the door to scold him in totally incomprehensible Russian while she mimed washing her hands and pointed at him.

'OK, Lyudmila,' he said, holding the hands in question up in a position of surrender. 'I'll go and wash my hands for dinner.'

As he turned to leave the room he threw a conspiratorial wink at the rest of them, suddenly reminding Penny of a mischievous schoolboy.

They were all rather subdued at the table that evening, in stark contrast to the usual buzz of conversation.

The news that, but for the lack of staff, they had the space available to give the programme a real boost was casting a real dampener on the friendly atmosphere which had grown up between them since she'd joined the team.

'It's just so frustrating,' Dare exploded as grabbed his serviette off his lap and flung it down beside his plate, his meal hardly touched. 'The longer those people are out in the community the more people they're infecting—and all for the want of nursing staff.'

He stood up suddenly, his chair making a ghastly scraping sound as it shot back on the polished wood floor. For a second it rocked precariously on its back legs before it settled back onto all four with a thud.

Dare had whirled away from the table to stride backwards and forwards in the limited space, the fingers of both hands raking through his hair as though he was contemplating pulling it out.

'What makes it even more difficult is the fact that we don't know the ins and outs of the local system,' Simon said. 'At least back home we know there's the possibility of calling in bank or agency nurses.'

'Even then, you've still got the same problem with lack of finance,' Maurice pointed out. 'No health authority would ever have enough spare cash sitting around to finance something as massive and unexpected as a TB epidemic *and* the implementing of a brand new system for combating it—even when the new system is going to save them money in the long run.'

'The other frustration is knowing that just a few years ago there were so many fully trained staff working here—before all the political problems upset the apple-cart. Unfortunately, they're not here any more so. . .'

Suddenly, Dare's words made a connection in Penny's brain, and she had to tune him out for a moment while she thought it through.

'Dare,' she interrupted urgently, 'I think. . .I might have the possibility of an answer.'

One dark blond eyebrow shot up towards his unruly hair and he folded his arms across his chest, as though he was armouring himself against accepting whatever she said, but she didn't allow it to deter her.

'I know it wouldn't be the solution to the whole problem,' she began, knowing that she sounded as if she was hedging her bets, 'but Olga was talking to me this morning and she was telling me about some of the nurses she used to work with at the hospital.'

'Were they some of the ones who left when everything started to fall apart?' Maurice asked.

'That's right,' she confirmed. 'They had worked here for fifteen or twenty years and really enjoyed their jobs.'

'So?' Dare challenged. 'They left because the pay and conditions had deteriorated. Since then nothing has changed so they're unlikely to want to come back.'

'Except that three of them are very good friends of Olga's, and she's been enthusing about what we're doing here with the DOTS programme. She told me that they haven't taken other jobs since they left the hospital because they wouldn't get the same satisfaction as they did from nursing. Added to that, they are bored out of their minds, staying at home.'

At this stage she decided not to bother explaining about Russian grandmothers—there would be plenty of time for that if anything came of her idea.

'Are you suggesting that they might want to come back to work for us? Without pay?' he demanded incredulously.

'I don't know,' she admitted honestly, then, when she saw the look of impatience crossing his face, hurried on. 'I only made the connection when you were talking a few moments ago. When I remembered what Olga had said about her friends I thought it might be worth exploring.'

There were several moments of silence as they all digested the idea, and Penny's eyes were going from one face to the other while she tried to gauge their response.

Simon and Maurice actually looked quite intrigued with her brainstorm, but Dare's thoughts were less easy to decipher.

'It's worth a shot, isn't it?' Simon suggested. 'We haven't got anything to lose.'

'It would be absolutely marvellous if they did agree,' Maurice butted in eagerly. 'If they're all as well qualified as Olga it would be a real shot in the arm for the unit. It would boost the number of patients we can treat during the trial and give us much more data to draw on when we present the results to their health department. That would virtually guarantee that the DOTS programme will be adopted!'

'Hold on, Maurice,' Dare cautioned. 'You're talking as if these nurses had already volunteered, and we haven't even approached them yet.'

'When will we do it, then?' Maurice demanded, obviously all in favour of the idea. 'Don't forget, there are twenty-one cases of active TB wandering around infecting other people, so the sooner we see where we're going. . .'

'I'll borrow Petr and have a word with Olga tomorrow,' Dare said, then paused when he caught sight of Penny's face.

'You disagree?' he challenged. 'I thought you were

the one who was all for it—it was your suggestion in the first place.'

'And, as such, I think *I* ought to be the one to approach her about it—after all, I work most closely with her and I'll be the one directing her friends if they *do* agree.'

For a second it looked as if he was going to argue the toss, but then he shrugged.

'Whatever,' he agreed. 'It'll probably be easier if you talk to her because there won't be so many problems with translation.' He grinned wryly. 'I'll have to let London office know how much I appreciate the fact that they chose a Russian-speaking nurse to send out as Melissa's replacement.'

Penny's heart fluttered briefly when she saw the gleam of approval in his eyes, and she found herself crossing her fingers superstitiously in the hope that her idea might be the seed that bore fruit. It would be dreadful if, after all this discussion and high hopes, it all came to nothing.

After that, the rest of the evening seemed rather flat. Maurice had his nose deep inside a thick paperback and Simon was scribbling away quietly at a letter.

The fact that he'd tucked himself in the chair in the corner to do it led Penny to speculate that he might be writing to a woman, but there was no way she was going to embarrass him by asking in front of the other two.

Penny had pulled out her knitting as she hated sitting without something to occupy her hands.

She'd started the back of a big sloppy jumper a couple of evenings ago and was nearly halfway up to the armholes already, still amazed that the colour of the wool she'd chosen exactly matched the colour of Dare's eyes.

She refused to speculate on the reasons why she might have chosen that particular colour. There was no way she could have known that she and Dare were going to end up working together in Nevansk, and she couldn't possibly have been thinking of the colour of his eyes when she went to buy the wool. . .could she?

It was a good job she could knit without keeping her eyes on her work all the time because it didn't matter how often she told herself not to watch Dare it seemed that just seconds later she was following his every move.

Like Simon, he'd started off by reading, his material a series of professional journals, but he'd laid them aside some time ago and was staring into the distance.

'The articles weren't as interesting as you thought?' she asked, then felt a flush climb up her throat and into her cheeks when the gaze he focused on her grew in intensity.

It was almost as if he was trying to see inside her head to find out whether she *really* wanted to know or was just making idle conversation.

'Actually, they were,' he began slowly. 'They're accounts of a couple of different avenues being taken in London and New York to develop quicker and cheaper methods of detecting TB and developing a method of testing the efficacy of a new generation of TB drugs.'

'It would certainly make things cheaper if there was a quicker way of doing the sputum tests. The one we're using now was first devised over fifty years ago, and I've known it to take up to ten weeks before we get a result.'

'This one is completely different. They're working on two different methods—one gets a result from a blood sample and the other is done as two skin injections.'

'And it would be cheaper?' Penny asked, as she dropped her gaze briefly to her work and looked up again, keen not to miss a single word as she watched the expressions crossing his intent face.

'They're still working to develop it for commercial use but, yes, it should be cheaper. More importantly, it'll be so much quicker.'

'What about the tests for the drugs?' Maurice asked, his book forgotten as he joined in the conversation with his own sphere of interest. 'Is that the one where they're trying to make the bacteria react like fireflies?'

'That's the one,' Dare agreed. 'They've—'

'Fireflies?' Simon chimed in. 'Did you say they're using fireflies against TB?'

There was a round of laughter.

'Not quite,' Dare said. 'They've introduced the firefly's light gene into the drug-resistant TB bacterium, and they've found that the light only switches on when the bacterium is resistant to the antibiotic they use to try to kill it. The whole thing takes only half the time of the old tests.'

Simon whistled. 'That'll make it so much easier for the drug companies to test new products.'

'I certainly hope so,' Maurice said. 'It's been so prohibitively expensive to do all the weeks of testing on every sample that drug companies have been very reluctant to do *any* research into new compounds for TB. The ones we're using now are nearly all the same, or just minor variations, of the ones we've been using for years.'

'Patients are always asking the nursing staff why it takes so long to get a result,' Penny added. 'They often think it's because the drug is slow-acting so we have to explain that it's actually the TB bacterium that takes so long to grow before there's enough of it to do the tests on.'

'That's another thing they're hoping to do with these new tests,' Dare continued. 'If they can make them sensitive enough they'll be able to give a result with as few as a hundred cells.'

The three male members of the team then embarked on one of their highly complex conversations, each of them drawing from their individual disciplines to stretch the others' minds with theories and possibilities.

Penny came to the end of a row and hesitated over starting another. In the end, she folded her work and put it away. Now would be a good time for her to go up and take advantage of the bathroom being free. She could have a shower and wash her hair before any of the men were ready to end their discussion.

Penny wrapped a large towel around herself and sighed luxuriously as she stepped out of the shower.

Mindful that there were three others to follow her, she'd been sparing with the hot water, but in spite of that the time she'd spent, standing under the spray, had been long enough to pummel her muscles and nerves into submission. All she had to do now was settle herself into her room for a soothing session with her hairdryer and she would be ready for bed.

She was humming softly as she leant forward to wipe the condensation from the mirror over the basin. She didn't know whether it was the sudden waft of chilly air, swirling through the steamy warmth of the tiny bathroom, or the sound of a stifled gasp which told her she wasn't alone any more.

She was certain she'd flipped the lock on the door,

but when she whirled around she found Dare poised halfway into the room, one hand holding the door open and his wash-kit tucked under the other arm.

Her sudden movement had jeopardised the safety of her precariously tucked towel, but when she tried to grab for the edges her hands seemed to be moving in slow motion, not nearly fast enough to prevent an increasing amount of heat-flushed skin being revealed.

The towel might have eluded *her* grasp, but one lean-fingered hand shot out in time to prevent her being left totally naked in front of him.

'Th-thank you,' she stammered as she tried to wrap the edges of the towel around herself again and came into contact with the hand, still preserving her modesty.

Suddenly she became very aware of the warmth of his fingers where they curled against her skin, his knuckles just brushing the inner curves of her breasts and sending a shower of sparks to travel right through her.

She tightened her grip on the towel but he didn't take any notice of the subtle hint that she'd regained control.

He seemed in no hurry to release his grasp, and finally his very stillness forced her to look up at him— to find his gaze silently riveted on her, apparently fascinated by her state of disarray.

Her breath froze in her throat as his eyes met hers, and for the first time she caught a glimpse of the emotions seething deep inside him.

She didn't know whether he was aware of the fact that the desire blazing out at her was hot enough to sear her to the bone, but it called to something inside her which she hadn't even known existed before this moment.

His eyes flickered down to her mouth and she felt it as keenly as if he'd touched her lips. She couldn't help giving in to the urge to moisten them with the tip of her tongue.

She heard him draw in a sharp breath and his own tongue emerged to mimic hers as he leant towards her.

He was going to kiss her, she thought, and was jolted by a deep twist of excitement, her lips parting again in anticipation and her eyes drifting closed.

'Have you nearly finished, Penny?' came Simon's voice through the door, simultaneous with his brisk knock.

The interruption was as shocking as a deluge of icy water.

Instantly, Dare straightened away from her, and she could have wept when she saw the way his expression had closed up again, his feelings once more hidden behind those impenetrable shutters as he gestured for her to reply.

'In. . .in just a minute,' she called breathlessly as she tried to fumble her way into her dressing-gown, without releasing her hold on the precarious towel.

She was all too aware that the door still wasn't locked and if Simon were to try the handle she and Dare would be caught in a very compromising situation.

'Hurry up, or I'll be beating the door down,' Simon threatened good-naturedly, and they heard his footsteps cross the corridor and fade into his room.

Penny whirled towards the basin and grabbed her wash-bag, frantically dumping everything into it without regard for neatness or the fact that the bag wouldn't close properly.

She was horribly aware that Dare had retrieved his

own wash-bag and was standing silently behind her, waiting for her to gather up her belongings.

'If you open the door you can tell me if there's anyone about,' he suggested in a hushed murmur. 'With any luck, Simon won't hear my feet. . .'

They were lucky.

Penny let out a sigh of relief when she saw that the hallway was empty, and she sped barefoot towards her room, her slippers clutched against her racing heart as she concentrated on reaching sanctuary.

At the last moment she remembered Simon and stuck her head back out of the door, just in time to see Dare disappear silently into his own room.

'Bathroom's free,' she called, and hoped she was the only one who could hear the way her voice was trembling.

'Stupid!' she hissed as she leant back against the closed door and shut her eyes in despair. 'Now he'll think you're *always* making an exhibition of yourself.'

She drew in a shuddering breath and forced herself to walk across to the small chest of drawers, which also served as a dressing-table, and dump her wash bag on it.

Immediately it tipped over and half the contents cascaded onto the floor, but she didn't care enough to bother to pick any of it up as she collapsed in a heap on her bed.

'First it was the evening dress without any underwear,' she groaned into her pillow as she hugged it to her chest. 'Now it's the forget-to-lock-the-door and lose-the-towel routine. He's going to think I'm a raving nymphomaniac!'

She wanted to scream, but she didn't think the pillow was thick enough to stifle that. All she could do was make herself concentrate on her breathing as she fought the desire to howl her eyes out, refusing to think about the reason his good opinion should mean so much to her.

In the end routine claimed her, and she uncurled herself from the centre of the bed to begin the task of combing out the knots from her half-dried hair.

When her grandmother had done it she had made it part of a routine which included stories about her own early life in Russia, interspersed with the fairy-tales her own grandmother had told her.

Usually the routine was soothing, helping her to unwind at the end of the day so that she could fall asleep straight away, but she knew it wasn't going to work tonight.

By the time her hair was dry and she was ready to go to bed she knew there would be no point in turning off the light and lying down—her head was too full of regrets and if-onlys.

If she had only remembered to lock the door Dare wouldn't have been in the room when she lost control of her towel. Until then she'd believed that they were beginning to build up a rapport—a solid appreciation of each other's skills and strengths. Now he'd been reminded, in the most graphic way possible, that his first impression of her had been of a promiscuous socialite.

That was *another* if only that she couldn't bear to dwell on—the one which made her wish that she'd remembered her parents' fundraiser in time. Then she'd have had the special underwear ready to wear under that wretched dress and Dare wouldn't have thought. . .

But—she sighed—if only was a phrase that could ruin a life, the sign of someone who couldn't leave the past behind, allowing it to cast a pall over the future.

She didn't have time for that. There was too much work to be done in too short a time, especially over the next six months, if they were to help persuade the Russian authorities to implement the DOTS system.

She would be working with Dare until they reached the end of the trial, and it was up to her to make sure that her behaviour was absolutely above reproach from now on. Eventually, Dare would realise that tonight's episode had just been an accident.

It had taken her over an hour, but she had finally rationalised her thoughts sufficiently so that she was able to turn the light out and settle down.

She'd been peripherally aware of the sounds of the others, taking their turn in the bathroom, while she'd tried to come to terms with what had happened, and now the house was quiet. She should be able to get some sleep.

Unfortunately, her subconscious had other ideas.

Almost as soon as she closed her eyes her imagination took over, conjuring up scene after scene—each more wildly erotic than the last and all of them involving Dare and herself.

By the time she heard Lyudmila arrive the next morning to start preparing their breakfast she'd been lying awake, staring up at the ceiling, for several hours—not daring to close her eyes.

She'd lost count of the times she'd woken during the night with her pulse racing and her whole body throbbing with arousal, her dreams supplying her with scenarios she'd never imagined possible.

Just thinking about them now, with the rest of the house stirring to life, brought a fiery blush to her cheeks.

'Thank God he's not a mind-reader,' she muttered

as she hurried into her dressing-gown and grabbed the pile of clothes she'd set ready.

She blushed again as she paused just inside the bathroom and checked a second time that the lock had caught properly, then hurried through her wash. The last thing she wanted was to meet Dare in the corridor when he'd just climbed out of bed. She could imagine how sexy he would look, his dark blond hair all rumpled and his jaw shadowed with a day's growth of stubble.

It was the thought of meeting his eyes for the first time since they'd nearly been caught together in the bathroom that was enough to make her fingers fly over buttons and zips, and she was out of the bathroom in record time.

It only took a couple of minutes for her to tidy her room and she was on her way downstairs.

She would need to have at least one cup of Lyudmila's *chai* inside her before she was ready for their first confrontation.

Dare heard Penny's footsteps going down the stairs and lay back against his bunched pillows, his hands behind his head. He knew she'd had a restles night last night because he'd been lying awake, listening to the sound of her tossing and turning.

In a strange way it had made his own insomnia more bearable...but it hadn't stopped him thinking about his reaction to her as she'd stood there in the steamy atmosphere of the tiny bathroom, her wet hair and freshly scrubbed face making her seem somehow innocent and defenceless.

He snorted quietly.

He'd known from the first time he'd seen her with her naked body barely covered by that slinky white dress that 'innocent' and 'defenceless' were the last words he would ever associate with her.

She was sophisticated, wealthy, free and easy with her favours and totally out of his league, but she was so heart-stoppingly beautiful that her unsuitability hadn't stopped his body from reacting in a predictably lustful way.

Nor did a resurgence of juvenile hormonal overload excuse his insane urge to kiss her last night, willing and eager though she had seemed to be.

Just thinking about the way her dark eyes had gleamed up at him, her lips parting sweetly to allow the flicker of her tongue to leave them glistening, tempting. . .

'Enough!' he groaned, and swung his legs over the edge of the bed. He stood naked in the early morning chill of the bedroom in the forlorn hope that it would have a cooling effect on his body as well as his thoughts. Six months of this, and he'd be a basket case unless he found some sort of control.

He needed to keep his distance from her.

He needed to control the attraction he felt for her because he knew better than anyone that it couldn't go anywhere—she might be a darned good TB nurse but, with her family background, it was more than likely that she would sooner or later be marrying some suitable man straight out of the same top drawer.

She certainly wouldn't be interested—not even as a short-term fling—in someone from the very bottom drawer who'd had to fight for everything he'd wanted.

Not that he was looking for any sort of relationship, short or long term.

It was three years since he'd lost Tess, and while their relationship hadn't been perfect he had cared about her. Had cared deeply, but that still hadn't been able to save her—

'Dare? Are you up?' Maurice demanded, his hearty voice cutting like a sharp knife through the dull ache of guilt and regret. 'Lyudmila said to tell you that breakfast's nearly ready.'

'I'm up,' Dare growled, with a wry glance downward at his single-minded body. 'Just going to dive under the shower and I'll be down.'

No need to broadcast the fact that it would be another cold shower—for all the good it had done him last night. He'd still lain there for most of the night, putting together the glimpses he'd caught of Penny's body and imagining what the rest of her would look like.

CHAPTER SEVEN

'YOU don't eat enough to keep a sparrow alive,' Dare accused harshly.

Penny had been playing nervously with her breakfast, not daring to look across at him for fear of what she'd see in his eyes.

The anger in his voice froze her in her seat, her hands clenched tightly around her cup.

'How can you expect to work properly if you don't start off with a proper meal?' he continued. 'You know as well as the rest of the team that good nutrition is essential in any sort of stressful situation—it's one of the basic ways of helping our patients to combat their TB, apart from making sense in everyday life.'

'Dare. . .' Maurice began warily, but when Penny glanced quickly up at him and gave her head a brief shake he subsided uneasily.

'I'm sorry, but I'm. . .a bit wound up about talking to Olga this morning,' she invented, and crossed her fingers guiltily under the cover of the table, still avoiding his gaze.

She'd only looked at him once, a lightning glance when he was the last to arrive at the table, his hair still shower-dark and bearing the marks of his comb, his jaw and cheeks so smooth they were almost shiny after his recent shave.

After that, she'd been careful to keep her eyes well away from him lest she broadcast to the whole group her growing fascination with the man.

'Are you worried about asking her? Would you rather I did it?' he offered.

It sounded like genuine concern but she didn't dare look at him to find out.

'No, it's not worry, exactly,' she said, frantically casting about for some way to get herself out of the corner she was rapidly creating, her eyes skittering everywhere around the room except towards the seat opposite her.

'It's more a case of. . .anticipation,' she invented, her voice warming to the idea. 'At times she seemed so lonely, and once she told me about losing her mother, and then her colleagues leaving, I could understand how isolated she was feeling. I can hardly wait to put the suggestion to her and see what she says.'

'If that's all it is,' he began, doubt clear in his voice, and finally Penny couldn't help herself—she just had to take a quick look at him to see what expression accompanied his voice. It sounded almost as if. . .as if he was concerned about her. . .

It was supposed to be just a glance, but once she looked across at him she became trapped in his deep blue gaze and her heart began beating like a frightened rabbit's.

His eyes were so dark they looked almost black, and so intent that he seemed to be able to look right inside her to the insecure young woman who hid behind the calm, confident façade of an experienced TB nurse.

Shaken, she dragged her eyes away.

It had been years since she'd allowed herself to think about that, years since she'd allowed herself to admit that the tug of war which had consumed her childhood—between her father's vision of her future and her own—still affected her.

Although she had always been able to count on her beloved grandmother's support, the whole situation had left her so emotionally insecure that she still automatically shunned any sort of close personal friendships with either sex.

Unfortunately, now that she found herself attracted to Dare she just didn't know how to behave.

She'd never been able to relax enough in the company of men to tease and flirt the way her contemporaries did. She'd never invited people home, male or female, knowing that her father was always going to have the last word on who were or weren't suitable companions for his daughter.

The first time she had actually dared to go directly against his wishes had been when she'd applied for a place to train as a nurse, and it had been her belief that it was what she'd been *meant* to do which had given her the determination to ride out the furore her decision had caused.

It was that same gritty determination which enabled Penny to talk brightly to Simon and Maurice on the way across to the unit.

She couldn't quite bring herself to include Dare in the conversation yet, but if she was lucky no one would notice that she was carefully avoiding looking in his direction.

In any event, by the time they arrived Olga was already in the unit, preparing for the influx of patients. With Maurice's murmured 'Good luck,' and Simon's raised fingers crossed for the same outcome, she drew in a fortifying breath and walked into the little treatment room.

'*Zdraste, Olga*,' she said with a smile, and gestured her over while she sat herself in one of the chairs.

'Did you wish to speak to me?' Olga asked warily

as she sat down on the very edge of the other seat.

'Yes. About the nurses who used to work here with you,' Penny said and then, seeing Olga's apprehension, hurried on to stop her worrying that she had spoken out of turn about the problems the hospital was having.

'Yesterday you were telling me about the nurses who used to work in the hospital with you, and the fact that they are bored, staying at home.'

'Ah.' The older woman smiled and settled herself more comfortably on the chair. 'I saw Lana last night and she said she was almost desperate enough to *pay* for something to do!'

'Do you think she would want to come back and work here—on a temporary basis?' Penny proposed.

'Of course! But. . .but here there was no money so there were no jobs,' Olga retorted with a puzzled frown. 'That is why she left. . .why they all left.'

'Well, there's still no money, but now there is a great need for some experienced nurses for at least two weeks—we would need all three of your friends to come in, if they were interested.'

Olga looked intrigued so Penny quickly outlined the hospital's provisional agreement to the MERLIN team's use of the nearby ward and their inability to provide any staff.

'You know that we have twenty-one more people needing the special care they'd get during the first two weeks of their treatment,' Penny continued.

'Also, if they are here, in the hospital, they will not be giving the sickness to any more people,' Olga added.

'Exactly, but we can only do it if we can find enough staff, willing to help us.'

Olga was already on her feet.

'When would you need to know? How quickly must I talk to my friends?'

'The sooner the better so we can work out what supplies we'll need,' Penny confirmed. 'Would you be able to contact them by phone, or do you think it would be better if you spoke to them in person?'

'If I could use the telephone to speak to Lana then she will be able to speak to Galina and Valeria straight away.'

Penny waved her on her way. Olga had already taken out the record cards of the patients who usually arrived first so Penny was able to promise that she could cope with any early patients until Yelena arrived.

She was on tenterhooks while she waited for Olga to make her call from the administration office, needlessly checking and straightening the containers of tablets and the patients' record cards just for the sake of keeping her hands busy.

Yelena wasn't due for another ten minutes and there had been no sound of the door into the waiting area opening to admit a patient, but suddenly she knew that she wasn't alone any more and whirled to face the intruder.

'Dare!' she exclaimed, with a hand clutched to her throat. 'You made me jump. I didn't hear you come in.'

'Sorry about that, but I couldn't wait any longer.' He glanced around. 'Don't tell me Olga hasn't come to work today!'

'She's here, but she's gone to phone one of her friends,' Penny explained. 'I'm waiting for her to return with the verdict.'

'Well, I've been on the phone, too—to London office.' As he spoke she was once again trapped by his intense gaze, almost mesmerised by the heat and energy he seemed to radiate.

'Is there a problem?' she asked, her voice sounding strangely distant to her ears as she concentrated on keeping her breathing even. The awareness she had felt towards him from the first moment she'd seen him—before she'd even been introduced to him at her parents' fundraiser—seemed to be growing at an alarming rate, no matter how determined she was to keep it under control.

'No. No problem, but I thought it would be a good idea if I found out if there might be some money forthcoming from MERLIN to pay these good women. It goes against the grain to ask them to work for nothing.'

'And?' Penny prompted, a warm glow surrounding her heart at Dare's concern for Olga's unknown friends.

He seemed such a self-contained man, so much in control of himself and disdainful of other less-focused mortals, but every so often he wasn't able to prevent her getting glimpses of his softer, caring side.

'And there's a good chance that they'll get something all the while they're working with us on the DOTS programme.'

'That's great news!' she exclaimed. 'Just wait till we tell Olga!'

'That's always supposing that her friends are willing,' he cautioned. 'And, even if it *is* forthcoming, it's not a great deal of money.'

'It's better than nothing and at least, if our pay is anything to go by, it'll be paid regularly.'

She'd dropped her voice to add the last part of the sentence in case there were any eavesdroppers, but as she hadn't seen either of their translators yet this morning it seemed fairly safe.

She was just beginning to wonder what had

happened to Olga when her familiar form came bust-
ling into view, just as the door to the waiting area
opened to admit the first consignment of patients.

'Drat,' Penny muttered, torn between wanting to
talk to Olga and needing to monitor the swallowing
of the drugs. Today there were blood samples to take
to check kidney function, too. . .

'Go and speak to Olga,' Dare prompted as he took
one of the seats behind the table. 'I can count out
tablets as well as anyone else.'

'But, unless you've magically mastered Cyrillic
script, you still need Olga to mark the cards for you,'
Penny pointed out with a chuckle. 'Even *I* need Olga
to find the records for me because my written Russian
isn't very good and there are several different sets of
handwriting involved.'

'OK,' he sighed as he stood again and conceded his
place to Olga. 'All I can tell from her smile is that
she's pleased about something.'

'The *Doktor* wants to know if your friends said
OK,' Penny asked cryptically, with a glance towards
their first waiting patient.

'*Da*, OK,' Olga said, with a broader grin than ever.
'They were all at Lana's house together, drinking *chai*
and feeling miserable, when I telephone, and they say
yes, yes, yes!'

Penny turned to Dare with a smile of her own.

'Do you need a translation?' she asked, knowing
from his expression that he had understood enough
from Olga's body language without needing to hear
the words.

'I just need to know how soon they can start so we
can get organised,' he said, his eagerness like a powerful force field around him.

Penny fired a couple of questions at Olga while the

older woman continued to flick rapidly through the file index to take out the record card for the first patient, then turned to Dare to relay her replies.

'She says that the three of them will need a couple of hours to let their husbands and families know what's happening, but they're hoping to be here straight after the midday meal so that they can find out all about what we're doing and what we need them to do.'

'They really are that keen?' Dare marvelled. 'Well, if they're half as conscientious as Olga is, I think we're on a winning streak.'

There was a definite spring to his step as he turned to make his way out of the room, turning at the last minute to blow a totally unexpected kiss in their direction.

'*Spacibo*, Olga. *Spacibo*, Penny,' he called, expressing his thanks with one of the few words he knew in Russian, then they could hear the eager sound of his swift footsteps recede along the corridor towards their newly extended domain.

Penny smiled wryly to herself.

That's the way it was going to be, was it?

Since breakfast he had been at great pains to avoid any trace of familiarity with her, making certain that their conversation was strictly limited to the work in hand.

There had been those brief seconds when their eyes had met and time seemed to disappear around them, but he hadn't allowed it to happen again.

Penny concentrated on marking in the next record card. She'd made a decision to keep some distance between Dare and herself so she could hardly complain if he had made the same decision—it should make the whole thing easier if they were both working towards the same end.

There was absolutely no reason why she should be surrounded by a creeping feeling of loneliness.

There was a barely suppressed air of excitement in the unit all morning, with the sound of much to-ing and fro-ing further along the corridor.

At odd moments each of them managed to sneak along to see how far the cleaning crew had got, and when it was time for their lunch break all of them lingered for the few minutes it took to make up the two long rows of beds with fresh linen, leaving the taller members of the crew to rehang the hastily laundered curtains.

Meanwhile, Dare had been busy.

First he'd had to ask for an electrician to be found who could install several of the ultraviolet lights which had travelled to Nevansk with Penny, then he began the mammoth task of trying to contact each of the patients on his list to ask them to report to the hospital the following morning.

Apart from maintaining her overall supervision of the drugs monitoring for their outpatients, Penny had also made herself responsible for checking their supplies of particulate masks and disposable gloves and aprons because she knew that the old-style ward was far less amenable to the specifics of true barrier-nursing.

Her consolation was that unless any of them had been unlucky enough to have been in contact with one of the drug-resistant forms of TB all of the patients would cease to be infectious after a relatively short time on the high level of chemotherapy they would receive.

Once they reached the dining room they discovered

that the hospital grapevine was just as efficient in Russia as it was in England.

The MERLIN team was besieged by questioners while they tried to eat their meal, ranging from the downright antagonistic few who totally disapproved of the hospital committee's decision, and accused the outsiders of trying to take over the whole hospital, to those who had already been convinced that the DOTS programme was the better treatment and were volunteering to help out for a few hours when they came off duty in the main part of the hospital.

At last the meal was over and it was time to meet Olga's friends.

'How are we going to work this? Do you want to give them the guided tour?' Dare asked as they all made their way back to the unit.

'It's probably going to be better if the three of them start off with Olga and we explain what we do in there,' Penny suggested. 'Then you and Yelena can take them through to meet Simon and Maurice and explain what *they're* doing before you finish up in the ward.'

'They're going to need more than a five-minute introduction to the system of record-keeping and the new central pharmacy,' Dare pointed out. 'You couldn't possibly expect them to absorb everything that quickly.'

'Actually, what I'd thought was that we could split them up when they actually start work so that one stayed with Olga to learn the ropes from her while the other two came through to the ward with Yelena and I. Then we could change around until each of them has been through everything thoroughly enough to know what they're doing and why.'

'That sounds like it would work,' he said approvingly. 'It will make certain that no one is left at a loose end and nothing is left undone.'

'It also means that you will be free to act as trouble-shooter,' she pointed out. 'I very much doubt whether the whole thing will get off the ground completely smoothly, and we don't want to upset the hospital authorities. Some of them are still very anti—'

'As they made certain we knew at lunch,' Dare supplied.

'*They're* the ones who'll make certain that we do everything strictly by the book,' Penny said, her concern colouring her voice. '*They're* the ones who would love to jump on something and use it as an excuse to discredit the new system.'

'I get your point,' he said with a wry expression. 'I've a feeling that the next two weeks are going to be a real trial by fire, but if we come out at the other side with another twenty or so patients safe to go back home while they continue treatment it could prove to be just the shot in the arm we needed.'

He surprised her by reaching for her hand and giving it a quick squeeze, the contact as electric as if she'd grasped a live wire with her bare hand.

He released her almost as soon as he'd touched her, almost as if he'd regretted his impulsive action, but the sensation lingered, her fingers warm and tingly for long moments after she'd self-consciously tucked them behind her back.

'One thing I'm not looking forward to is getting to grips with the contact tracing,' Dare continued, and Penny realised that she must have been wrong. He was so unaffected by the brief connection between them that he was able to shove his hand casually into his trouser pocket, hooking his white coat back to

display an enviably flat stomach and long lean legs—
not that she was looking, of course.

'It's bad enough when we're dealing with half a
dozen at a time,' he continued, unaware that her concentration had wandered briefly before she dragged it
back under control. 'And it can be especially difficult
when they work in a large factory, with many people
working closely together—the number of tests we
have to do to eliminate the majority and identify the—
hopefully—small number of affected people.'

'And all of it taking place in a country where you
don't understand the language,' Penny added.

He shrugged.

'I'm not a linguist. There was never enough money
to allow us to travel when I was a child. Anyway,' he
added with an enigmatic smile, 'in the places I've been
since I qualified as a doctor the inhabitants haven't
exactly been proficient in the major European languages.'

Penny was just about to ask him what he meant
when Olga leapt to her feet with a glad cry.

'They're here,' Penny translated as three clones of
Olga advanced towards their friend with arms outstretched, their words tumbling over each other so fast
that Penny was completely lost.

Eventually the introductions were made and the
three women eagerly hung on Olga's every word while
she explained what the MERLIN team was trying to
achieve with its comparative trial of the World Health
Organisation's DOTS programme against the hospital's tried and tested traditional methods.

'They've been very quick to grasp the necessity for
meticulous record-keeping,' Penny commented in an
aside to Dare. 'But, most of all, Olga's done a fantastic
job as a one-woman sales force, both here and when

she was talking to them the other day, and they're really keen to help us implement the new system.'

'Olga's worked so hard to recruit the three of them that it's a shame we can't give her a productivity bonus,' he joked, but Penny took him seriously.

'I think we have,' she commented with a meaningful glance in Olga's direction. 'Have you ever seen her looking so alive, so animated before?'

'Something certainly seems to have given her a boost,' he agreed. 'She looks a good ten years younger than I thought, and positively bubbly with excitement.'

'I think she's been very lonely without her friends around, and you've just given them back to her.'

'Well, I'll be removing them again while I take them off for their tour, then I'll bring them back here,' Dare said, straightening off his perch on the corner of the table. 'I think it would be a good idea if the whole team met up at the end of the afternoon for a strategy-planning meeting and to answer any questions—on both sides.'

'Fine,' Penny agreed with a smile. 'I'll tell Yelena so she can translate to your flock of starlings while you're on your way to visit Simon and Maurice. See you later.'

She couldn't help watching him as he waited for the three women to stop chattering, a patient smile on his face as he leaned one shoulder against the doorframe.

The impatient man she'd believed him to be when she'd first met him would have been chivvying them along. The *real* Dare Campbell recognised that the four former colleagues were far too excited for anything as mundane as mere timekeeping.

'*Tovarishi!*' Penny called with a laugh in her voice, finally taking pity on the man. 'The *Doktor* is waiting to show you around, then you will come back here later!'

There was a round of laughing farewells and a brief salute from Dare before their little department was quiet again.

'Now we must check up on our patients,' Penny said briskly to Olga in an attempt to bring her feet back down to the ground. 'They'll be wondering what's going on with all this noise and laughter.'

'I think tomorrow they will all be gone,' Olga predicted with another of those sweet smiles which were rapidly becoming a permanent feature. 'Then we will only see them when they come for the medicines.'

'I'm certain we won't be left idle when they're gone,' Penny said. 'There are twenty-one sets of contacts being traced to see if our new patients have infected anyone else since they developed the active disease.'

'And if they are lucky there will be room for them to be treated in *our* department,' Olga said with her new-found fervency.

Penny smiled. It was hard to remember how suspicious Olga had been of the DOTS system and how ready to praise the traditional medicine which her hospital had been delivering for decades. If the team needed anyone to beat the drum for them with the Russian authorities they couldn't do any better than Olga Tereshkova.

There was a special atmosphere in their borrowed house that night.

Lyudmila seemed to have picked up on the day's excitement and the meal had turned into an impromptu celebration.

She'd produced a bottle of Crimean wine to go with

the meal, like a magician pulling a rabbit out of a hat, then, instead of the usual *chai* at the end of the meal, had ceremonially carried out a small silver tray with a bottle and four fragile etched glasses.

'Azerbaijani brandy,' Penny translated when the little woman flapped a hand at them as if they were chickens, shooing them ahead of her into the sitting room. 'According to Lyudmila, it's eminently better than anything the French make!'

Penny wasn't really keen on drinking spirits, but she couldn't disappoint their beaming housekeeper and settled on one end of the settee with a small quantity of the dark amber liquid in the bottom of her glass.

The four of them talked easily as they wound down from the frantic activities of the day, while Lyudmila finished her tasks in the kitchen.

A little later she stuck her head round the door to deliver a smiling '*Dos vidanya!*' before she left for the night.

'She was right about this brandy,' Maurice commented in approval as he offered a refill around the room. 'I would never have connected a place like Azerbaijan with the production of something like this.'

'You're right,' Simon agreed. 'When all you see are those newsreels of death and destruction you don't think of what the country was like *before*, when people were able to get on with their lives.'

'Even more so when you've seen it happening,' Dare said quietly, his gaze fixed on his own glass.

There were several seconds' silence while everyone absorbed what he'd said.

'You've been there?' Simon demanded. 'With MERLIN?'

'Yes,' Dare said after a pause which told Penny that he regretted his slip of the tongue.

Perhaps it had been the result of the relaxed atmosphere over the meal, or the brandy which followed, but she was certain that he hadn't intended telling any of them of the experiences which had put that grim tone in his voice and the shuttered expression on his face.

'When were you there? Was it with a team like this, or were you in the vanguard with the assessment team?' Simon prompted, obviously not going to let it go at that.

For a moment, when he put his unfinished glass down with a less than steady hand, Penny thought Dare was going to get up and leave, but in the end he just planted his elbows on his thighs and linked his hands between his knees, leaning forward to stare at the well-worn carpet.

'It was several years ago when there was all that trouble in Armenia,' Dare provided, after a telling pause. 'MERLIN put a team in Nagorno Karabakh to carry out inoculations. The children were so malnourished they were in a worse state than those in Bosnia.'

The tone of his voice told them of the sights he had seen, without a word of description.

'We were there for three and a half months and travelled to three different centres to inoculate over six thousand of the under fives against diphtheria, tetanus, polio, measles and whooping cough.'

'So how did you end up in Azerbaijan?' Maurice asked, his usual genial smile hidden by a frown of concern.

'The team was just finishing the distribution of emergency medical stocks to refugee centres and hospitals throughout the region and we were getting ready to leave. Then we had a call, telling us about the quarter of a million refugees who had fled into

Azerbaijan from Nagorno Karabakh. The reports said they were living in the open without proper food and shelter.'

For a moment it looked as if he wasn't going to say any more, but then he continued, his voice sounding as if every word had been dragged over gravel.

'Throughout our three months in the region there had been intermittent bombardment going on, and we'd been lucky to avoid most of it. But just after I left one member of the team was hit by shrapnel and... and died.'

'Oh, man...' Simon groaned as he shook his head. 'One of the people you'd been working with?'

Dare nodded silently, his gaze fixed on the fingers he was gripping so tightly together that his knuckles showed bone-white through the skin.

He didn't say any more—didn't even look up at them—but Penny knew there was something more to it than he was saying.

Had the person who'd died been a colleague before they'd travelled out with MERLIN—someone he'd known for a long time? Or was it someone he'd formed a particular friendship with while they were in Nagorno Karabakh—a woman, perhaps?

She was startled by the swift twist of jealousy which pierced her, drawing her breath in sharply before she could control the reflex.

Dare heard her and glanced in her direction with a questioning look in his eyes, but she dropped her gaze to the empty glass she was still cradling between her palms.

'Well,' she said huskily, and drew in a deep breath before she allowed it to escape in a silent stream while she counted and waited for her voice to steady.

'It's going to be a very long day tomorrow,' she

began again, more successfully this time, 'so I'm going to grab the bathroom first, if no one objects.'

There were murmurs of agreement from Simon and Maurice, accompanied by subdued smiles, but a dark silence from Dare as he raised one dark blond eyebrow.

His eyes said it all.

She didn't need to hear him speak to know what he was thinking, and she felt the heat bloom over her face and neck.

But he wasn't the only one who couldn't forget what had happened when she'd neglected to lock the door properly, and while she couldn't go back in time to wipe out what had happened at least she'd learned her lesson—she double-checked the wretched thing every time now.

What she couldn't do was double-check a lock on her memory, which insisted on replaying the events of those few minutes—the heat of appreciation and desire in his eyes as he'd looked at her scantily clad body, and the moment when his head had bent towards hers, his lips parting as he prepared to kiss her.

If only she could lock away those memories, and the heated dreams which had followed, she might stand a chance of getting a good night's sleep. She had a feeling that tomorrow was going to be a nightmare.

CHAPTER EIGHT

'I KNEW it was going to be chaos,' Penny muttered to Yelena halfway through the morning. 'I just didn't know how bad it was going to be.'

'It wouldn't be so bad if the patients had turned up alone,' Yelena said. 'Unfortunately, their families have heard a bit about what's going on here, and they've all used it as an excuse to come and have a look at us.'

'*That's* why I've been feeling like a prize exhibit at the zoo, is it?' Penny quipped, then reached out swiftly to bar the way into one of the isolation rooms when someone wearing ordinary street clothes went to open the door.

She tried to explain to the suspicious gentleman exactly why he couldn't just wander in for a visit, but her Russian wasn't up to it and she had to concede to Yelena's fluency.

Even so, it took several minutes for Yelena to persuade the man that they weren't hiding anything— that there were no terrible tortures being carried out in secret behind closed doors.

In the end, she gave him some leaflets about the DOTS programme, specially translated into Russian, and he went off quite happily to report back to the patient he'd arrived with.

'Have you seen how our new members of staff are getting on?' Penny asked. 'I've barely had time to speak to them this morning. They've really been thrown in at the deep end.'

'And they're loving every minute of it—they're as happy as children let loose in a sweetshop.'

Penny chuckled. 'Isn't it strange what some people's idea of fun is? I don't think you'd get many nurses volunteering to work in this sort of chaos, but those three are acting as if we're doing them a favour! I hope we get the word soon about how much we'll be able to offer them in pay because that'll really put the cherry on the top for them.'

'Penny?'

Dare's voice cut through their light-hearted relief from the tumult surrounding them, and the urgency in his voice had her whirling to face him.

'Problem?' she demanded briefly as she obeyed his beckoning finger and followed him swiftly towards her little office.

'Big problem,' he said, with a fierce scowl. 'We've just found out that one of the new intake is a teacher who works in one of the primary schools.'

'Oh, no!' Penny groaned.

'Which school?' Yelena demanded from the doorway, having assumed, quite rightly, that he had something serious to report. 'Do the hospital authorities know?'

'Petr has informed them and they've decided, in view of everything going on here, that they're going to send a team out to the school to check numbers and names.'

'Oh, Lord!' Penny exclaimed, torn between her desire to go and the knowledge that she was needed more in the unit.

'I presume that the hospital is insisting on taking this over?' she continued, her mind working at a million miles a minute. 'Will they let one of the MERLIN team go too, and, if so, who can we spare? Simon's going to be awash with samples in the lab, I'm up to my eyes here and Maurice is starting to pull his hair out in the pharmacy.'

'That's what I thought,' Dare admitted with a wry expression. 'I'm the least necessary here, it seems, so I asked Petr to suggest to the powers that be that the two of us went—I thought it would help to keep us in the good graces of the hospital if they didn't have to lose another member of staff, knowing how pushed they are.'

Petr arrived with the hospital's acceptance of Dare's offer, and it didn't take long to stuff Dare's emergency medical pack with the extra supplies he'd need.

They still had no idea yet of the numbers involved, but as she watched them leave Penny found herself superstitiously crossing her fingers that it was a very tiny class in a very small school.

There wasn't time to stand around, she reminded herself with a swift mental shake. She had close to thirty inpatients to supervise, three staff who—while they were excellent nurses—were still learning the ropes as far as the DOTS system went, a constant trickle of patients arriving for their next dose of chemotherapy and a multitude of extraneous bodies of all ages, wandering around at will.

That was something she needed to change— quickly.

'Right, Yelena, it's time to wield a big broom,' she declared with the light of battle in her eyes.

'A broom?' the younger woman questioned. 'You wish to sweep something?'

'Yes,' Penny said decisively. 'I wish to sweep out all these bodies who are getting in the way in our unit. They have had plenty of time to deliver their relatives, and now it's time for them to go.'

'You are right,' Yelena declared, straightening her shoulders. 'This is a hospital, *not* a zoo!'

The two of them grinned at each other and then, shoulder to shoulder marched into their new domain and began, politely but firmly, to evict all the stray bodies.

It took nearly an hour before the last of them had been sent on their way, but then the real business started.

'I *must* go and check up on Olga and her partner for a minute, Yelena,' Penny said, suddenly realising that it had been ages since she'd left the older woman in charge of administering the drugs and updating the outpatients' records, as well as teaching her friend what to do.

'So I shall start her two friends in here to take a full case history of each of the new patients and take samples to send to Simon in the lab.'

'That will be wonderful.' Penny smiled. 'I also need to find out whether the hospital kitchens know that the population has just had a minor explosion or the poor souls will be at their wits' end, trying to stretch the supplies.'

'They know already,' Yelena said calmly. 'Someone came up while you were filling the *Doktor's* bag so I told them how many more were here.'

'You're wonderful!' Penny said with a laugh. 'I wouldn't want to have the patients' relatives accusing me of starving their loved ones.'

Gradually everything began to calm down until order reigned, helped in large measure by the expert efficiency of Olga's friends.

It was Valeria and Galina who had drawn ward duty, and they were obviously nurses of the old school—the type who knew their job inside out and did it perfectly, and could probably demand instant obedience from junior nurses and recalcitrant patients alike with nothing more than a stern look.

The difference was that the two of them were so obviously enjoying being back in harness that they couldn't help grinning at each other and the patients.

There was no doubt that several of the new intake were quite seriously ill, and most of them were making copious use of the sputum pots. The heartening thing was that, over the space of that first day, the overall atmosphere in the ward changed from one of gloom and despair to one of cautious optimism.

It could have helped that Yelena had finished making the brightly coloured posters for the outpatient area and had 'stolen' some of them to put up on the freshly scrubbed walls in the ward but, mostly, Penny thought it was the attitude of the staff ministering to them.

She started wondering what Dare would think of all they'd achieved in such a short time, and pulled herself up short—she'd realised that there was no prospect of a relationship with him and had made a rational decision not to allow herself to grow attached to him.

Unfortunately, just because she was kept busy, and Dare wasn't around, didn't mean that Penny stopped thinking about him.

There was only time for a short lunch break, but she missed the chance to see him and listen while he talked to the other members of staff.

She was also imagining what he had found when he'd arrived at the school. Had the teacher been ill for a long time, coughing over his vulnerable charges day after day and risking their health and their lives?

Were many of them infected?

How many?

And how many of them were already seriously ill, without knowing it?

The thoughts were running round and round inside her head, giving her no peace because she knew she wouldn't find out any of the answers until he returned.

At one point she heard the sound of a siren and looked out of the window in time to see an ambulance, speeding away from the hospital, but she could only guess what that had been about.

One thing she was delighted to be able to do was confirm to the six patients in the isolation rooms that they were ready to go home to their families.

Dare had signed their releases just before they had found out about the children, and now it was time for a pep talk to reinforce the message about the importance of finishing the course of antibiotics.

'We have your record card here,' she told each of them in turn. 'You must come back three times a week to take your tablets and have them marked on your card, then you can be sure that you will stay well.'

Olga had added a few words of her own, warning them of the dire consequences if they should stop taking the drugs too soon, but at present they were still too grateful that an imminent death sentence was no longer hanging over them to think about letting their chemotherapy lapse.

'We will see how many of them remember my words when they forget what it was like to sweat at night and cough their hearts out,' Olga said with gritty realism. 'What they don't know is that I won't *let* them forget. They must not let this illness become resistant to drugs or it could kill millions.'

Lana was quite wide-eyed at her friend's vehemence, and Penny couldn't help wondering exactly how much MERLIN's advent in Olga's life had changed her.

She certainly wasn't the same person she'd been when Penny had first been introduced to her, the dour, forbidding expression apparently gone for ever, but she'd changed even more in the last day since her friends had rejoined her on the staff.

'I like your hair that way, Olga,' Penny said to test out her theory, gesturing towards the pretty combs holding gleaming sweeps of hair up at each side before the rest was coiled neatly away into a dark crown.

'*Spacibo*,' Olga said, with a hint of added colour in her cheeks. 'Galina gave these to me for a birthday gift when we were all working here before, and I had forgotten about them for a while.'

Penny smiled, glad that she had paid the lonely woman the much-needed compliment. There was definitely more to her than met the eye.

As there was with the tall athletic figure who was just striding into the unit.

Penny's heart gave an erratic thump as she caught sight of Dare but she ruthlessly subdued the reaction as she walked swiftly towards him.

'What did you find?' she asked when he was still halfway across the room. 'Do you think he's infected any of them?'

'Unfortunately, yes,' Dare said grimly. 'Several at least. One of the class was too ill to be at school today so we had to go to her family home. She's in a bad way—it looks like it could be tuberculous meningitis.'

'Oh, Lord. The poor child,' she breathed. 'How bad?'

'Acute. There's still a possibility that it's bacterial meningitis and nothing to do with the tuberculosis but, from the few tests I had time to do on site, she was showing odd cranial nerve and long tract signs, apart from being drowsy and complaining that her head hurt.'

'How are you going to find out which it is?'

'We're going to have to examine her cerebro-spinal fluid, and we'll need blood samples, too.'

'Do you want her in one of the isolation rooms?' Penny suggested. 'All six are empty now.'

'Ideal,' he said shortly. 'I came on ahead of the ambulance, but she should be here any moment.'

Olga was busy for the moment so it was Yelena who helped Penny check the preparations in the negative-pressure room.

'It will be very frightening for a little girl,' Yelena commented when they switched on the high-powered extraction fan and closed the door behind them.

'It sounds as if she will be too sick to care,' Penny replied, her head coming up sharply when she heard the sound of heavy feet coming along the corridor.

The two burly men, carrying the stretcher between them, absolutely dwarfed the slight figure huddled under the blanket between them.

'*Zdraste*,' one of them muttered through his mask as they arrived, then followed the direction of Yelena's pointing arm.

'She's so little,' Penny said with a catch in her voice as they settled the little girl gently into the high bed and raised the safety bars at either side.

'Only six years,' supplied one of the ambulancemen gruffly, obviously just as affected by the frailty of his charge as she was. 'Just a baby. . .'

He turned away and walked swiftly out of the room, his tough appearance at odds with his soft heart as he tried to hide the suspicious moisture gathering in his eyes.

'How is she?' Dare demanded as he entered the small room, one hand occupied with shaping the top band of the special particulate mask over his nose, his eyes deeply blue against the stark white.

He took the departing ambulanceman's position beside the bed just as Penny jotted down her initial set of observations on the child's chart.

'Her temperature's raised and she's so drowsy that she's almost comatose—barely responding at all.'

'Can you get a CSF tray in here so we can get a sample of fluid off to Simon? We need to get a move on because it's going to take three hours to get a result on it as it is.'

Yelena stayed in case she was needed to help with the procedure, usually a wise precaution when a young child couldn't be relied upon to stay still for the potentially dangerous procedure.

In the event, Natalia was too ill to fight when Penny positioned her on her side to curve the slender spine into a tight arc.

Moving swiftly, Dare cleaned and anaesthetised the region over the junction between her third and fourth lumbar vertebrae and positioned the needle to pierce the sheath surrounding the spinal cord.

'First time,' Penny heard him mutter on a relieved sigh as the fluid began to flow through the needle as soon as he withdrew the stylet.

He held his hand out for the first of the four tubes they would need, and Penny placed it in his hand.

'Done,' he said as he straightened. 'Now, let's get the blood sample and the whole lot can go to Simon.'

It was the work of seconds for him to draw up the necessary volume of blood, and as soon as the cap was on the sample Penny peeled the last label off the strip Yelena had prepared and stuck it in position.

'Can you take these straight up, Yelena, and make sure that they go straight into Simon's hand?' Penny cautioned. 'He should be all set up and ready to start work on them.'

'In the meantime,' Dare said as he reached for a fresh syringe, 'we need to start her on maximum chemotherapy—rifampicin and streptomycin—and she'll need corticosteroid cover to reduce the meningeal inflammation.'

Once the drugs were administered there was little they could do for the little child, other than try to make her comfortable.

Penny was loath to leave the child's side, as if standing over her would help the chemotherapy to do its work better, but she had other patients who needed her and a vastly enlarged unit to organise.

'As soon as Yelena comes back from delivering the samples to the lab I'll get her to special Natalia for a while,' she murmured, feeling the puff of her words directed back at her by the particulate mask covering the lower half of her face.

'Fine,' Dare replied, his own voice similarly muffled. 'I'll be backwards and forwards at odd times, but I want to find out what's happened to the rest of those children.'

'You think they might have been allocated to the other side of the hospital?' Penny asked, and turned aside to strip off her disposables, hoping that her voice hadn't revealed the way her heart had sunk at the idea.

'It's a possibility,' he conceded grimly, his eyes darkening over the edge of his mask before he dragged it away and balled it up with the rest of his contaminated clothing.

'Well, if they're having difficulty finding space for them over there you can let them know that we've got five more isolation rooms empty,' Penny offered eagerly, wanting the youngsters to have the best poss-ible chance of recovery and believing wholeheartedly that the DOTS system would provide it.

'But how would you staff them?' he demanded, his voice apparently roughened by concern. 'We've had to draft in three of Olga's friends to deal with the new ward, but with the best will in the world they can't do everything—and neither can you.'

'I've got plenty of spare time on my hands in the evenings,' she pointed out. 'It's not as if I'm involved in a wild social life. . . And, anyway, several of the staff on the other side volunteered their time when they finished their official shifts. I'm sure Yelena would remember who they were and would know how to contact them.'

'Right. I'll bear that in mind when I get over there,' he promised. 'But, first, I must find out the latest situation.'

The rest of the afternoon was exhausting.

It wasn't just the sheer physical effort involved in organising and taking care of so many inpatients, but the fact that every few minutes she found herself wondering what was happening in the main part of the hospital.

How many children had they decided to hospitalise?

How sick were they?

What sort of treatment were they going to be receiv-ing—the traditional Russian methods or their own more quickly effective DOTS?

There had been a minor panic when the first of the patients in the new ward had passed water and had discovered that their urine had turned red. They had been so overwhelmed by what was going on around them that they hadn't listened properly when they'd been warned about this side-effect of the rifampicin.

'Well, it won't do you any good to cry about it,' she pointed out to the worried patient, 'because your tears will be the same colour!'

The gist of her humour was rapidly passed around the long old-fashioned ward and drew appreciative chuckles from those well enough to follow what was going on.

Luckily, they hadn't had any other side-effects from the drugs so far, but it wouldn't be long before her overworked staff were going to have to add another task to their duties—taking blood samples to check for damage to their patients' kidney function.

'Swings and roundabouts,' she murmured under her breath as she removed more sputum pots for rapid disposal. 'You can't have a drug that's so effective against something like TB without some sort of side-effects. . .'

As the afternoon wore on she'd had to send a message over to Lyudmila to warn her that no one knew when they might be finishing work tonight. It would be unfair if the elderly woman had gone to her usual trouble to prepare a delicious meal and then none of them turned up for it.

Suddenly Dare was there—at the head of a small procession of wheelchairs.

Penny couldn't see his face for the mask he was wearing, but the sparkling brilliance of his eyes was enough to tell her that he was smiling.

'Can you help me to hide three victims of kidnapping?' he asked, his voice hushed as if he were plotting some sort of conspiracy.

'Dare!' she squeaked in horror. 'You didn't really kidnap them, did you?'

'You'd have thought I was trying to, the way some

of the medics over there reacted when I made your offer.'

'So, what happened?' she asked as she led the way into the smaller corridor between the six specially converted rooms.

'We've obviously made a good enough impression on some of our Russian colleagues that they stood up for us and suggested the children be allowed onto our programme, but the clincher was when they pointed out that it would save the hospital money if they were treated out of *our* budget rather than theirs.'

'Hit them where it hurts—in their pockets!' she joked, then her smile faded as she turned towards the frightened-looking little band and her heart went out to them.

They were so young—the oldest eight and the youngest only five.

'*Zdraste, tovarichi,*' she greeted them, careful to speak slowly enough so that any deficiencies in her accent would not prevent them from understanding her.

'My name is Penny,' she continued. 'I come from England, but my grandmother came from Russia so I came to Nevansk in a big aeroplane to help look after you.'

She signalled to the porters to wheel each of the chairs forward to one of the rooms.

'Each of you will have a special room,' she began again, only to be interrupted by the oldest boy.

'Just a minute, please? We have a room each? Not together?' he questioned, pointing from himself to a younger boy with very similar features. 'Always at home I have to sleep with my brother, and he keeps me awake. He wriggles!'

There was a tentative laugh from one of the other

children, and a half-hearted denial from the
younger boy.

'Well, now he can wriggle all he likes because he's
got a bed all to himself, too! Shall we all go and look?'

She sneaked a quick look in through the glazed
panel and saw Yelena, bending over Natalia's still
form, but she couldn't stop now. She had this little
band to settle into their new quarters, with case histories to write down, samples to take and fears to calm.

'Well done,' Dare murmured and she turned to face
his smiling eyes over his mask. 'I don't know what
you said to them, but they seem much happier now.
Of course, that could be a disadvantage when they're
feeling better because they'll probably try to run the
lot of us ragged!'

'But it'll be worth it to see them behaving like
normal healthy kids, won't it?' she retorted, with an
answering smile.

'Anything I can do to help?' he offered.

'Nothing yet, thank you. I'd rather get them settled
in their own rooms before we start sticking needles in
them for samples or the first one to cry will set the
lot of them off.'

'Good thinking,' he said, and she could see the
rueful look he threw her, even with the mask covering
a large portion of his face.

'You could go in and check Natalia for me,' she
said, with a quick glance over her shoulder towards
the first room in the row. 'I don't think Yelena's very
happy with her progress.'

He saluted her silently and crossed the corridor,
leaving her to her new charges.

Considering the age of her young patients, some of
the case notes were a little lacking in details, such as
their precise dates of birth, but Penny wasn't worried.

She knew that by the morning their complete medical histories would be available.

The thing which worried her more was the fact that none of their parents had wanted to stay with the children, and she resolved to enlist Yelena's help in finding out why.

They were so very young to have to lose contact with their families in such a strange and frightening environment.

She had her chance sooner than she had expected when a nurse from the other side of the hospital arrived a little while later to take over from Yelena and give her a break from her observation of Natalia.

'Do *you* know why none of the parents wanted to stay with the children?' she asked as she stuck her head around the door into her little office where Yelena was sipping at some piping hot *chai*, then turning to lean her aching back against the doorframe for a moment.

'Probably because they are afraid that they will carry the illness back to the rest of their families at home,' she said quietly. 'Many of them have to share apartments with too many family members, and when one is sick they are afraid all will be sick and they will not be able to work to pay rent, buy food.'

'But they are so young and so frightened,' Penny objected. 'Don't their parents love them?'

'*Da*! Yes!' she retorted indignantly. 'Russian people love their children very much, but when the doctors tell them that the whole family might catch TB they will believe it and let the doctors do their job to make them well again.'

'Perhaps I need to send those doctors a translation of the research which showed how much faster children recovered when their parents were with them in the hospital,' Penny suggested pugnaciously. 'Poor little things, they shouldn't have to be—'

'Penny! Calm down,' Yelena advised in exasperation. 'You cannot change the doctors' minds in one night. All you can do is take care of the little ones and send them home as soon as possible.'

'But—'

'Just think,' Yelena continued with a persuasive smile. 'They have been allocated to the DOTS system so they should be out of here in about two weeks, rather than nine months or a year.'

'I'm sorry. You're quite right.' Penny subsided with a self-deprecating grimace. 'It's just that I can't bear to see them cry themselves to sleep.'

'Well, my replacement, sitting in with Natalia, just told me that Olga's gang heard about our youngest TB victims. Apparently, they have been in contact with some more of their old colleagues and they are organising a "voluntary granny force" to help look after them.'

'A *what*?' Penny laughed.

'They are all trained nurses and most of them have had children and grandchildren so they will be coming in as if they are just ordinary visitors, but they can help with the ordinary nursing jobs, as well as helping to keep them entertained.'

'Oh, Yelena, that's a wonderful idea!' Penny said, her eyes prickling with the threat of emotional tears. 'I have always been told that Russia is a land which values grandmothers, but I thought it was just my own grandmother, trying to bang her own drum.'

'And now you know *why* we value them,' Yelena pointed out as she stood up, ready to return to her little charge. 'They are very powerful, very hard-working people within the family, helping to keep the generations together by sharing the responsibilities and acting as a. . .a cushion between them.'

'My *babushka* certainly did all of that, *and* made certain that she annoyed my father at least once a day!'

'That, also, is part of their job!' Yelena said with a laugh. 'Now, do you want me to go back in to Natalia's room to continue observing?'

'No, Yelena, you deserve a break from that— you've been sitting in that hard chair long enough,' Penny decided. 'Would you like to do a quick tour around the new ward to see that everyone is settled?'

Her young colleague threw her a smile of agreement and set off along the corridor.

Penny had hardly taken two paces towards the steady hum of the pressurised particulate filters, running in each of the isolation rooms, when Natalia's door swung open and the volunteer stuck her head out and looked both ways.

'*Sestra!*' she called as soon as she caught sight of Penny, beckoning her to come quickly.

Penny quickened her pace until it was only just less than an outright run, an awful feeling causing her heart to sink towards her eminently practical shoes.

CHAPTER NINE

PENNY glanced at herself in the mirror and groaned. She'd splashed her face with cold water and even held a cold flannel over her eyes, but she still looked like a Technicolor panda.

She sighed and blew her nose—again.

This wasn't like her at all. She'd never been one to burst into tears, no matter what the situation—her father had taught her too well.

But when she'd hurried into Natalia's little room earlier this evening, her hands still busy fastening her particulate mask as she leant back against the door to close it behind her, the first thing she'd seen had been that frail little body convulsing in the middle of that enormous bed while Dare had tried to prevent her from hurting herself still further.

She'd taken over his job, trying to shield her little charge from hitting the protective rails on either side of the bed, while he sought to stabilise her, but all to no avail.

'Is she reacting against the chemotherapy drugs?' Penny asked, desperate to find some simple reason for this awful situation—something as easily remedied as changing the drugs she'd been started on for one of the variations available.

'I wish that was all it was,' he muttered darkly.

There was anger in his voice, but his expression was shuttered as he flicked the beam of his penlight into the little child's unresponsive eyes.

'Unfortunately' he continued, his calm control back

152

in place again, 'it looks like the TB is winning this battle. It had too good a hold before we found out about her. . .'

By the end of another hour she was dead, her tortured little body finally at peace.

'I know it was the kindest thing for her,' she whispered to herself as she sat in the darkness of a Siberian night in the middle of her tumbled bedclothes and hugged her long nightdress tightly around her legs, her forehead resting wearily on her knees.

Logically, she knew that Dare had done all the tests, and had given Natalia all the treatment he could.

Logically, she knew that the tuberculous meningitis must already have been too far advanced when she was diagnosed for any treatment to have made any difference to the outcome.

Logically, she knew that even if the fragile little girl had survived such a severe attack of the illness its very complexity would have ensured that she was permanently severely brain damaged and prey to increasing bouts of convulsions.

But that still didn't stop her wishing that poor Natalia had been diagnosed earlier—before the TB had erupted into her brain and taken hold so swiftly and disastrously.

The six-year-old's death had affected all the staff who had become associated with their little unit, from the core MERLIN team to the newest 'honorary grandmother' volunteer.

She had been the first patient to die since they'd set up the unit, but they had all been saddened that even *one* had been lost.

In the back of her mind she could hear her own dear grandmother's voice telling her, the way she often had, how important children were.

'*Every* child matters,' she had said fiercely when she had seen the televised accounts of famines and genocides around the globe. 'You never know which one has been destined to bring the world the cure for cancer or the way to lasting peace. They are our future. . .'

Thinking about the indomitable old lady made Penny think about the way her grandmother used to brush her hair. . .how soothing it had been during her childhood after yet another argument with her father about her tomboyish ways or her 'unfortunate' choice of friends.

She reached across to switch on the little bedside lamp with its old-fashioned parchment shade, and slipped off the bed to pad across the room barefoot to retrieve her brush.

She hadn't realised just how icy the floor was, scampering back swiftly to curl her feet under her as she settled onto the end of the bed.

Slowly she began to stroke the bristles through the long unruly strands, straightening and smoothing them from the crown of her head and down halfway to her waist.

If she closed her eyes she could almost imagine it was her beloved *babushka* who was brushing it for her, the liquid vowels of her native tongue flowing over Penny like a benediction, while she told stories of her own past, and spun tales of Russia's history and folklore.

Her hand stilled when she thought she heard a soft tapping at her door, her eyes flying to her little travelling clock to confirm that it was after midnight.

She shook her head, certain that she was imagining it. After the hectic day the team had just endured she knew she must be the only one left awake.

The tapping started again, so softly that whoever was doing it was being very careful not to wake the rest of the household.

'Yes?' she hissed softly as she slipped off the bed, her bare feet whispering almost silently across the floor towards the door. 'Who is it?'

'It's Dare,' came the hushed voice through the darkly polished wooden panels. 'Are you all right?'

She barely heard the question through the sudden clamour of her heart when she realised who was outside her door.

It didn't seem to matter that she was determined to maintain a proper distance between them—the man standing just a few inches away on the other side of the door was the only one who had ever had this effect on her and, if her clamouring heart was to be believed, the only one who ever would.

As if in a dream, she saw her hand reach out towards the handle, turn it and pull it towards her to allow a narrow wedge of buttery light to fall across the tall man standing in the darkness of the corridor, his haphazardly tied towelling robe forming a deep V to frame his broad naked chest

'W-what's the matter?' she whispered, trying desperately to ignore the muscles gleaming like polished bronze and the way the light gilded the thicket of dark golden hairs stretching from one nipple to the other.

She forced her eyes upwards to scan his face, trying to decipher the reason he'd knocked. 'Are you ill?'

The corners of his mouth lifted in a wry smile.

'That's what I came to ask *you*,' he said softly. 'I saw your light on, and after this evening. . .I was worried about you.'

Warmth stole around her heart at his husky admission and brought a smile to her lips.

There was the sudden sound of noisy bedsprings along the corridor, as though someone had suddenly turned over in bed, and Dare glanced briefly over his shoulder into the pitch darkness towards Simon's and Maurice's doors.

'I think we might be disturbing them,' Penny whispered, and opened the door a little wider to beckon him in with the hand still holding her forgotten hairbrush.

Dare seemed to hesitate a moment, but he stepped into the softly lit room and pushed the door closed behind him.

It wasn't until she heard the click of the latch that Penny came to her senses and realised what she'd done.

It was the middle of the night, she and Dare were the only ones left awake and she'd just invited him into her room when she was less than fully dressed.

Somehow the trepidation she expected to feel didn't materialise, especially when she saw the way he was looking at her, his eyes apparently mesmerised by her hair.

'I didn't realise there was so much of it,' he murmured with a gesture towards the long shining strands.

'I was just brushing it,' she said, shrugging self-consciously when she realised that Dare's proximity and the chill of the room had combined to tighten her nipples into hard little buds.

She was afraid they would be all too visible as they pressed against the soft fabric of her nightdress and wanted to fold her arms defensively around herself, but realised in time that such a move would only draw attention to her physical reaction.

'S-sometimes I think it's a lot more trouble than it's worth and I swear I'll have it all ch-chopped off,' she stammered, frantically trying to fill the electric silence stretching between them.

'No!'

As if he couldn't help himself, his hand came up to touch the long strands which framed one side of her face and fell over her shoulder towards her breast.

'How could you *think* of cutting something so glorious?' he demanded huskily as he rubbed the strands between his fingers, openly savouring its silky smoothness, before he lifted his eyes up to meet hers again.

For a moment she stood there, mesmerised like a doe caught in a car's headlights, and she watched the deep blue darken still further as his pupils dilated with awareness.

He took the single step needed to bring him close enough to touch her—close enough for her to detect the fresh clean scent she'd come to recognise from his soap and shampoo—and still she couldn't look away.

'You've been crying,' he murmured with a frown.

She pressed her lips together and drew in a shaky breath, suddenly remembering the heart-wrenching events earlier on that evening.

'Natalia?' he guessed, and she nodded.

'Oh, Penny,' he said on a sigh. 'You'll burn yourself up if you let it get to you like this. You won't be able to function.'

Penny knew he was right but there was no way she could admit to it, afraid that, like her father, he wouldn't tolerate any display of weakness.

'I don't see you sleeping very soundly either,' she countered dryly. 'Or are you usually a nocturnal creature, like Count Dracula?'

He inclined his head in admission, conceding her point. 'It doesn't happen often,' he murmured, 'but. . . It's the children that get to me. Every one of them is so precious, every one of them has so much potential inside them that you sometimes wonder what marvellous things they're capable of achieving during their lives. . . And then to see all that snuffed out by a bullet, or a bacterium. . .' He shook his head.

Penny stared up at him, wide-eyed, as a shiver worked its way up her spine, her brush falling from nerveless fingers onto the small circular rug at her feet.

It was almost as if he had been listening to her thoughts earlier when she'd been remembering what her grandmother had told her. The similarity was uncanny. . .

'Dare?' she murmured, her voice all but strangled in her throat by the swift beat of her heart as she realised a deeper similarity between Dare and her beloved *babushka*.

As she gazed up at him it was as if a veil had been torn from her eyes.

Of all the people in her life, she'd loved her grandmother most for her gentleness and quiet wisdom and for allowing her to be who she needed to be.

Now there was Dare in her life, and suddenly she realised exactly how much he had come to mean to her, how he had found a place inside her heart which was deeper and wider than she could ever hope to express—and when she realised just how precious he was to her tears threatened again.

'Shh,' Dare whispered as he speared his fingers through her hair to cradle her head between his palms.

His thumbs stroked gently under each eye, catching the tears before they could spill over, then he leant towards her. His warm breath teased her lips as they hovered for tantalising seconds.

'Dare. . . We shouldn't—'

'Shh,' he repeated softly. 'We've both been wondering about this. . .about what it would be like. . .'

Her hands came up between them, but whether she'd intended to push him away she couldn't remember because as soon as they found the heat of his bare flesh between the open edges of his towelling robe she ceased to be able to think at all.

Unbidden, her hands turned until her palms were pressed flat against him. One small corner of her brain briefly registered the novelty of the whole experience, but the rest of her mind was totally occupied with revelling in every nuance of the warmth and width and strength of his powerful body.

Before her fingers had done more than stir the silky strands which covered him thickly from one side of his chest to the other he'd pressed his lips fiercely over hers, a deep groan resonating through his chest and into his throat.

He opened his lips over hers and took possession of her mouth with his tongue and his teeth, duelling with her in the sweet darkness and exploring her depths with a rhythm that tormented her with its mimicry.

He stilled and drew back slightly, but she couldn't bear the thought that their kiss had ended so soon. Her fingers tunnelled through the thick strands on the back of his head as she tried to pull him down to her again.

'Ah-h, Penny, I can't do it,' he groaned, as he wrapped both arms around her fiercely and held her tight, his face buried in her neck.

'C-can't do. . .what?' she questioned faintly as her heart sank.

She'd never known a kiss like it—had never wanted a kiss like it—but now that she had tasted the magic of Dare's kiss she wanted more. . .she wanted everything.

And he didn't want to continue?

Hesitantly, she began to drag her hands away from

their exploration of the shape of his head, dreading the moment when she would have to meet his eyes and see what a naïve fool she'd shown herself to be.

She drew in a shaky breath, not certain that her legs would carry her when he let her go. . .not wanting him to let her go at all.

'It's no good,' he said with a touch of anger in his voice. 'I thought I could kiss you once, just to satisfy the need that's been burning in me ever since that fundraiser, but I can't do it. I can't kiss you once and let you go. . . Not now that I've tasted you. . .held you. . .'

Time stood still as she tried to understand what he was saying, her brain only seeming to work at half-speed.

'You. . .you want me?' she ventured, finally daring to look up into the dark sapphire of his eyes—knowing that she would see the truth there.

'God, yes!' he groaned as he opened both hands wide on her back and caressed her from her shoulders to her waist and beyond, pulling her tightly against his body to show her the proof. 'Why do you think I've been finding any excuse to be near you—to work with you? Why do you think I've been so bad-tempered?'

'You mean that's not your normal mood?' she dared to tease, her heart soaring.

'No, dammit, it's not,' he retorted. 'I'm normally the most even-tempered of men—when I can get a good night's sleep—but ever since you appeared in my life I've been trying to exist on catnaps and dreams.'

'Well. . .'

She hesitated, her courage wavering until she saw the heat in his gaze, then she swallowed to clear the nervousness from her tight throat.

'Perhaps you'd like to find out if your sleeplessness is just due to sleeping in the wrong bed?' she asked, with just a hint of a quiver in her voice. 'Perhaps you'd like to see if you can sleep better in my bed?'

'Penny, if I come into your bed it won't be because I want to sleep, and I certainly wouldn't be letting *you* get any sleep. I would need to make love to you all night long just to take the edge off the desire I feel for you.'

'Well, then, perhaps you'd better get started,' she said with an attempt at bravado totally at odds with her lack of experience. 'I wouldn't like you to be late for breakfast.'

He gave a husky laugh, his eyes shining with devilment as he bent to sweep her off her feet and carry her to the bed—as if he couldn't bear to stop touching her.

'Oh, Penny, love, that sounds suspiciously like a challenge to me, and I've never been able to ignore a challenge,' he murmured roughly, as he slid his hands down her sides to grasp a double handful of her nightdress and draw it up over head in a single sweep.

Penny gasped in surprise when she was left wearing nothing but her panties, and her hands rose reflexively to cover herself from his heated gaze.

'Don't,' he whispered, catching her wrists in his long-fingered grasp to draw them away. 'The panties are a blow to my fantasies, but. . .let me look at you, please. . .'

As his eyes travelled over her their gaze was as potent as the touch which followed. She could see that he liked what he was seeing and all her inhibitions faded away, her eyelids growing heavy when his hands followed where his eyes had led.

Penny revelled in the way her breasts rose under his appreciative exploration, her nipples tightening between his fingers and begging for a more thorough exploration. But he was moving on, his hands shaping her waist and hips and drawing her last small item of clothing away to fall at her feet.

She shivered, as much in reaction to his feather-light touch as to the chill of the room.

'You're freezing,' he muttered, and he quickly stripped the tumbled covers back on her bed. 'Get in and I'll warm you up.'

'Is that a promise?' she asked as she smiled up at him, bolder now that she was under the covers and able to watch the efficient way he shed his own clothing in a heap beside the bed.

She felt her eyes widen in awe when she finally saw him in all his naked glory and heard him chuckle.

'You're very good for a man's ego,' he murmured as he slid in beside her, his body hot enough to sear her as the narrow bed forced them to come into close contact from the first moment. 'That look of appreciation is enough to make any one of us think we're something special.'

For a moment she nearly blurted out that the only naked males she'd ever been this close to had been her patients, but some small voice of caution held her tongue.

'But you *are* something special,' she said truthfully as she revelled in his heat and closeness, but then he rolled towards her, pinning her under the lean weight of his aroused body.

'You're the one who's special,' he said in a husky voice as he glanced down at her, and her eyes followed the same path to see the way her breasts were partially flattened under his chest, her nipples hidden in the silky thicket of dark blond hair.

'Ever since I saw you wearing that damned evening

dress I've been thinking about you—even dreaming about you—wondering if you always go around without underwear—wondering if you could possibly be as beautiful, as sexy as I remembered. . .'

His voice died away, leaving her whole body throbbing with anticipation as he cupped her chin in one lean hand and tilted it up for the first of a feast of kisses, and the time for words was over.

Now it was time to feel, to taste, to savour, to possess and be possessed as he taught her, for the first time, what it was to be a woman.

Her heart was still pounding and her lungs fighting to remember how to breathe when he raised himself up on his elbows to fix her with a stern look.

'Why didn't you say something?' he growled, his own breathing still too heavy for normal speech.

'About what?' she said, unable to meet his eyes as she tried to bluff her way out of a conversation she didn't really want to have.

'About the fact that it was your first time,' he said with studied patience as he tilted her chin up to force her to look at him. 'If I'd known I could have made it better for you.'

Penny giggled. 'If you'd made it any better for me they'd have to name a new comet, streaking across the sky over Siberia!'

She saw his unnecessary concern dissolve into humour and just a touch of pride.

'That good, eh?' he asked with a boyishly self-conscious grin.

'Well, it's difficult to say,' she began with mock gravity, 'bearing in mind the fact that I haven't got any basis for comparison—but as soon as I have I'll be sure to let you know.'

'Well, my dear girl, if you want to perform a comparative study you have only to say the word. I'm perfectly willing to assist in whatever way I can,' he declared, as he slid his fingers over curves and hollows, which were still exquisitely sensitive. 'Never let it be said that a serious attempt at qualitative and quantitative research failed for want of volunteers. . .' And he captured her rosy nipple in his mouth and began the journey to ecstasy all over again.

There was a delicious novelty to waking up in the early hours of the morning wrapped in Dare's arms, Penny thought as she peered up at the tousled head sharing her pillow.

They'd fallen asleep with the bedside light still on, too sated and exhausted to summon the energy to reach for the switch.

Now the light was falling over his handsome features, delineating the width and height of his forehead and his straight nose and casting shadows under his thick eyelashes.

He looked younger somehow, and well rested in spite of the fact that neither of them had slept much.

She felt a smile creeping across her face when she thought how silly he would think her if he woke up and found her gazing at him with a moonstruck expression on her face. Then she realised that she didn't care how silly she looked—she had fallen in love with him and needed to lie here quietly, absorbing the delight of being so close, before he woke up and she had to hide her feelings.

'How long have you been awake?' he murmured, his voice still rusty with sleep.

'How did you know I was awake?' she countered

as she propped herself up on one elbow and leant over him. 'Your eyes are still closed.'

'I can feel you looking at me,' he whispered as he trapped her head and pulled it down for a long leisurely kiss.

Penny was ready in an instant for him to take things further, eager to continue her education in how to please him, but he drew her head down onto his shoulder and wrapped his arms around her.

'Why?' he asked into the still of the early morning. 'Why hadn't you been to bed with anyone before, and why now—why me?'

'Because I'd never wanted to before,' she replied simply, unashamed of the truth.

'For years now my father's been lining up the eminently suitable sons of his business friends for me, but there was no spark of interest with any of them and I wasn't going to settle for anything less than the sort of relationship my grandparents had.

'In fact,' she continued with brutal honesty, 'when I didn't fancy any of them as husbands and refused to hop into bed with them, in spite of their connections, some of them accused me of being frigid. . .and I was beginning to think that they were right.'

The accusation had hurt at the time, but she could laugh at it now.

'Take it from me, lady, you are *not* frigid,' Dare said fervently. 'If there were any *more* sparks of interest between us we'd set the house on fire!'

Penny chuckled, happy to hear him confirm again that the interest went both ways.

She had spent so many weeks trying to deny her attraction towards him—right from their disastrous first meeting—that it was both a relief and a cause for excitement that she could now allow herself to think about the relationship they had started to build, and to wonder where it would lead.

Slowly she began to realise that Dare wasn't so relaxed any more, a tension tightening his body so that she almost felt as if she was intruding on his personal space by leaving her arm wrapped around his waist.

'I got married five years ago,' he said suddenly, the words stark in the quiet of the room, and Penny felt as if she couldn't breathe, her heart and lungs crushed by a fierce blow.

'You. . .you're *married?*' she gasped in shock.

'No, I'm. . . Oh, God, no,' he said, gripping her tightly when she tried to fight her way out of his arms, pain at his betrayal making her frantic.

'I'm sorry, Penny,' he said hurriedly as he held her still. 'I didn't realise it sounded like that. She's gone, Penny. Tess is dead.'

The pain in his voice got through to her where his words couldn't, and she finally understood.

'Dead?' she repeated in horror as she gazed up at him.

'We were working together on the same MERLIN team in Nagorno Karabakh, but we decided that she shouldn't go to Azerbaijan with me. She was going to come back to England because we'd just discovered that she was pregnant.'

He didn't say any more, but Penny was able to put the last pieces of the puzzle together herself.

'She was the team member who was hit by the shrapnel, wasn't she?' she asked softly, not needing his nod to confirm it.

'Oh, Dare, I'm so sorry. It must have been a chance in millions that she would be injured, and as for dying—'

'I should have been there for her,' he said fiercely

through gritted teeth, his dark blue eyes filled with anger directed solely at himself. 'If I'd been taking care of her, instead of racing off being the hero—'

'She would probably still be dead,' Penny said, gripping his shoulders as if she was going to shake him. 'Or you would have died instead, leaving her to bring up your baby alone.'

'Either way, I should never have gone off without her. I should have made sure she was safely on her way home.'

'Oh, Dare,' she murmured, and wrapped her arms around his shoulders, knowing he would never allow himself to be comforted while he thought he was responsible for his wife's death.

The ensuing weeks were gruelling, with so many patients to care for and the contact tracing process turning up more and more.

But their magical nights together made everything worthwhile.

At first Penny had been shy of letting the rest of the team know that she and Dare were sleeping together, but after the third cramped night in a row he took unilateral action.

'My bed's bigger than yours so I had Lyudmila move your things into my room,' he announced as they opened the door to their borrowed home that night.

'You. . . Dare! You had no right to do that without telling me. What on earth will she think? And Simon and Maurice. . .'

'We'll think it's about time,' Maurice said with a wink as he stuck his head out into the hallway. 'It's hell on my nerves waiting to hear Dare tippy-toe across the landing before I can nod off—like waiting for the other shoe to drop!'

Penny felt her face turn scarlet, and her embarrassment wasn't helped by Simon's delighted laughter. But once she'd thrown cold water on her face and calmed down a bit she came down for her meal and found that the topic had been closed.

Lyudmila had the last word when Penny carried the final dishes out to the kitchen and was enveloped in a hug.

'*Atleechna*,' she murmured with a smile, and Penny was finally able to admit to herself that everything was indeed excellent.

CHAPTER TEN

THE first group of patients in the long borrowed ward had been signed off as fit to continue treatment at home and, as the hospital authorities had predicted, there had been another, equally large group waiting to take their places.

The difference this time was that the agreement so grudgingly given before was this time eagerly given.

'I think we're making some headway,' Simon declared cheerfully as they sat down in the sitting room that evening after another of Lyudmila's delicious meals. 'I actually saw one of the real hardline professor types from the other side in deep conversation with one of our off-duty volunteers at lunch today.'

'That was Viktor,' Maurice said. 'He dropped in to the pharmacy later on to tell me all about it. Apparently, he was being given a real grilling about how well our patients were doing in comparison with theirs, how much money he thought we were managing to save per patient and the average cost per patient of the chemotherapy.'

'If we can't convince them that the DOTS regimen is best medically, perhaps we can get at them through their pockets,' Penny quipped with a smile.

'Except our success rate knocks theirs into a cocked hat as well,' Dare pointed out.

'Hang on, though. The figures would be very different if this was an area where the multi-drug resistant strains of the bug were about,' Simon warned. 'It would cost a heck of a lot more per patient in drugs and long-term hospital care if that happened.'

'That's why my part of the team spends so much of its time reminding the patients how important it is that each of them completes their course,' Penny butted in. 'That's the *only* way we're going to stop that happening here.'

'They're lucky Nevansk isn't a popular holiday destination,' Maurice said with a grim frown. 'In some areas, it's the HIV-positive incomers who've brought the TB with them. In others areas, it's the incomers who catch TB from the poor people they encounter on their exotic holidays, and when they go back home for treatment they think they know better than the doctors and give up their treatment as soon as they feel better, leaving the damn TB resistant to anything we can throw at it.'

'And, having ridden his hobby-horse to a standstill, we declare the race a dead heat,' intoned Simon, holding an imaginary microphone to his mouth as if he were a commentator at a race meeting, and they all laughed.

Penny had been yawning for the last half-hour and finally couldn't keep her eyes open any longer.

'It's no good, everyone. I'm off to bed,' she announced as she rolled up her knitting.

'Is that your cue to disappear, too, Dare?' teased Maurice, and had a spare ball of wool thrown at him for his cheek.

'Talking about clues to disappear,' Simon began with a cheeky grin, 'a little bird told me that a certain pharmacist has been disappearing into corners for quiet chats with our Olga!'

'She's helping me to learn Russian, and I'm teaching her some English,' Maurice explained uncomfortably, looking as if he wanted to sink through the floor, and Penny had to take pity on him.

'Well, she's certainly a very different person to the one I first met—her friends have been dragging her off shopping, and that new hairstyle of hers, with the pretty combs, makes her look quite glamorous.'

Maurice threw a look of gratitude her way, but it was Dare who took over the conversation.

'Actually, I was wondering if there was any way we could predict which of the patients would have an adverse reaction to a particular group of drugs,' he said, his forehead pleated into a frown. 'We've had several of the latest intake who can't tolerate the rifampicin, and I've had to put them on ethambutol instead. Is there any way of checking to see if they have any factors in common?'

'What sort of thing do you mean? Blood group, or previously acquired antibodies, or do you mean to look at the stage the disease has reached by the time they start treatment, or the site of the disease?'

The conversation was off and running, and as the three of them went at it hammer and tongs, sharing ideas and suggestions, Penny smiled and set off up the stairs.

When she'd first joined the group she would have stayed down to join in the discussion and thoroughly enjoyed herself, but for the last couple of days she reached this time of night and she could hardly keep her eyes open.

In fact, now that she thought about it, she hadn't been feeling quite right for a week or more, and her period must be due soon if her tender, aching breasts were anything to go by.

She had a quick shower and pulled on her long

nightdress before she slid gratefully between the chilly sheets.

Not that the old-fashioned flannel garment would stay on for very long once Dare came to bed—he had a definite preference for cuddling up to her with nothing to prevent them touching from head to foot.

The cold bedclothes made her nipples tighten in self-defence, and the sensation was almost painful, prompting Penny to search out her diary to find out exactly when her wretched period was due.

'Soon, I hope, if it stops me being so tender,' she muttered, then pulled a face at the thought of having to explain to a man for the first time why they couldn't make love the way they usually did, before curling up together to sleep.

A month late? she mouthed silently as she saw the evidence in the absence of a circle on the approximate date. She wasn't ever completely regular, but how could she not have noticed?

She flicked back through the pages and tried to remember why she hadn't thought about it before, and stopped when she saw the tiny heart she'd drawn in the corner of the day she and Dare had first made love.

It was just a silly memento and wouldn't mean a thing to anyone else but—

Suddenly frantic, she started counting, forwards and backwards, desperate to make the numbers add up differently—but she couldn't.

Her heart was pounding in her chest as she tried to deny her conclusions, and she counted up to ten in English and Russian.

But nothing would change the fact that the first night she and Dare had made love—the only night they had made love without protection—she had conceived his child.

She blinked rapidly, not knowing whether the threatened tears were of joy or fear, and huddled in a tight ball under the bedclothes while she waited for Dare to come to bed.

'Hey, sleepyhead!' murmured a deep husky voice in her ear, and Penny prised her eyes open just far enough to look up into Dare's gleaming blue gaze.

'What time is it?' she mumbled, and closed her eyes again to snuggle into his arms, revelling in the newly familiar intimacy.

'Time for my morning kiss,' he announced with a wickedly intent chuckle in his voice as he teased her with his bristly chin. 'And I think I should get two today as you were too sleepy to give me my goodnight one last night.'

Penny's eyes popped open in surprise.

'It's morning already?' she squeaked, trying to avoid contact with his stubble.

'Yes, but very *early* morning,' he confirmed suggestively, sliding his hand up her side to cup her breast through her nightdress.

It was the uncomfortable tenderness which suddenly made her remember the conversation she'd hoped to have with him last night, and she bit her lip, trying to think of some way to introduce the topic.

'What's the matter?' he asked softly when she didn't respond to his caresses with her usual eagerness. 'Still too sleepy?'

'Um. . . Actually, Dare, I'm. . . They're a bit tender at the moment. . .and I. . .' she said awkwardly, feeling a blush stain her cheeks.

'Ah,' he said and drew his hand away, sliding it around her waist to turn her into the sheltering curve of his body. 'It's a pity, but a little restraint won't hurt—in fact it'll probably build up the anticipation for when you are ready.'

Penny sighed at his thoughtfulness when she realised that he thought her period had arrived, but she didn't feel up to contradicting him and was completely at a loss to know how to broach the topic on the tip of her tongue.

'Tess had a bad time with her periods,' he said quietly, his words stirring the fine hairs at her temple. 'Sometimes it helped if I rubbed her back, the way they tell you to do for women in labour.'

'Mine aren't usually that bad,' she murmured through the thunder of her anxious heartbeat, hoping that the fact that *he'd* brought the topic up meant that he was willing to take the conversation about his wife a little further.

'When she found out the baby was on the way, was she worried that her labour might be bad too?'

'I don't think she'd thought that far ahead,' he said sadly. 'We'd only just started to come to terms with the fact that she was pregnant.'

'Were you pleased?' she asked, feeling as if she was treading on eggshells and glad that their relative positions prevented her from looking at the expressions on his face when he spoke about the wife and child he'd lost. She wasn't certain she could have borne it if she had seen the evidence that he still loved them.

'A bit shocked at first because the pregnancy was accidental,' he admitted, 'but, yes, we were pleased that we were going to be a family.'

'And have you ever thought—'

'I don't think I'd feel the same way now,' he added sombrely, cutting across the most important question.

'The whole direction of my life has changed since then.'

'In what way?' she prompted, with her heart in her mouth. Perhaps he would tell her what she needed to know, without her having to ask.

'Well, *then* I was happily married and we'd volunteered for a six-month stint with MERLIN. After that we were going to concentrate on our careers for a couple of years before we thought about starting a family. *Now* a wife and family wouldn't fit in with my life any more—there's no telling where I'll be from one trip to the next.'

'But. . .' *But what about me*? her heart cried. *What about us?*

'At least I learned my lesson with Tess,' he murmured, almost as if he was talking to himself. 'I won't be letting myself get that close to anyone again—won't let myself care like that. I can't—it hurts too damn much when you lose them.'

Penny lay perfectly still, afraid that if she moved she would shatter as easily and completely as he had just shattered her dreams.

They'd been such simple dreams of loving and caring for the man she'd fallen in love with—the only man she'd ever cared about—and now the father of her child.

She'd spent such magical nights with him over the last few weeks, sharing and loving and being loved, and now he was telling her that it could never last—that he wouldn't *let* it last because he couldn't risk the pain of losing her.

She thought fleetingly about the ideas she'd had that the two of them could travel together on his endless odyssey to the world's disaster areas, and gave a mental shrug.

That could never happen now.

He'd all but told her that he didn't want her with him, and he obviously hadn't even thought of asking her to stay.

Anyway, even if he did, she wouldn't be able to agree—she could never risk the baby.

Surreptitiously, she slid her hand down to cover her stomach, trying to imagine what it would feel like when it was swollen with an active bundle of arms and legs.

She ached with the need to tell him about the miracle they'd created between them, and even drew in the breath to give voice to the words hovering on her tongue, but at the last moment she couldn't do it.

When Dare began speaking again it was obvious that his thoughts had moved on, too.

'We're different, Penny,' he said, as though musing aloud. 'Ours is a special partnership—we work well together, play well together—we've got the best of both worlds. . .'

'And when MERLIN flies us out of Nevansk?' she prompted softly, unable to resist.

'I don't think *you'll* have a problem finding a post. You might even be able to go back to your hospital in the East End of London and do what you do best— take care of your patients and encourage them towards health—and I'll go on to the next hotspot.'

Her heart clenched at the finality of his words. It didn't seem as if he was even contemplating contacting her when he returned to England periodically. . .

For one desperate moment she actually thought of telling him about the baby, regardless, but that madness passed almost as soon as it arrived. She could never live with herself if she knew that she had used a baby accidentally conceived to trap him into staying with her.

Penny lay quietly watching Dare as he climbed out of bed, the sight of his deliciously muscular body having its usual effect on her pulse and breathing, but this time her reaction was mixed with the pain of impending loss.

She drew in a shuddering sigh as he left to go to the bathroom, and lay staring up at the ceiling while she tried to sort calmly through her options.

Now that she'd realised that she was pregnant she knew that she couldn't stay here much longer without Dare finding out about the baby.

Just this morning, when she'd turned over in bed, she'd noticed a faintly queasy feeling, and she realised now that she would have to leave Nevansk before she suffered any full-blown attacks of morning sickness.

Her mind was whirling with all the things she would have to do before she could arrange to leave Siberia, while her heart was trying to persuade her to stay just a little bit longer.

She hadn't noticed that she'd been unusually quiet over breakfast until Dare caught her hand and gave it a squeeze.

'Do you need any painkillers?' he murmured quietly, a solicitous look on his face.

'N-no. I'm all right,' she muttered, guilt bringing heat flaring into her cheeks. There and then she realised that she would have to leave as soon as possible.

Dare had presumed that she hadn't responded to him this morning because her period had arrived, but how many days' grace would that give her?

It wasn't that she didn't *want* to make love with him—she did, desperately—but she couldn't be certain that her overflowing heart wouldn't trigger floods of tears that she had no way of explaining.

In the end it had all been frighteningly easy.

The phone call to MERLIN, requesting that she be released as soon as she could be replaced, brought the welcome news that Melissa's injured leg had healed and she was available again.

'Your timing couldn't be more perfect,' the long-distance voice said. 'We've got another delivery of drugs ready to ship out in four days so Melissa can travel out on the transport with them and you can take her seat on the return journey.'

Four days!

She thanked her and hung up the phone, her heart wrenched as she realised that there was no turning back now.

All she had to do now was tell the rest of the team of her decision without breaking down.

'You're leaving in four days?' Dare exclaimed, his voice rising with disbelief. 'Why?'

Penny couldn't meet his gaze, certain that when she saw the way his deep blue eyes were spitting fire at her she would burst into tears.

'Leave her alone, man,' Maurice advised quietly. 'She wouldn't have done it without a damned good reason. She's probably just exhausted and needs a break—she's been working her socks off here.'

There was a moment's silence, as if Dare was waiting for her to confirm Maurice's suggestion, but she didn't speak.

'Well, did they say they were sending someone out to replace you?' he demanded, exasperation clear in his voice.

'Yes. Melissa's fit again and she'll travel out with the next batch of drugs on the RAF transport, then—'

'Melissa's coming?' Simon exclaimed with unexpected enthusiasm. '*When* is she coming? She didn't tell me when she wrote. . .'

His voice tailed away when he realised that they were all looking at him in surprise, and his face reddened furiously, clashing horribly with his red hair.

'Oh-ho!' Maurice pounced, eager to exact some revenge after all Simon's teasing over his growing friendship with Olga. 'So *that's* who you've been sending all those letters to, is it?'

Penny breathed a sigh of relief as the byplay between Simon and Maurice took the attention off herself.

She still had some thinking to do and some decisions to make, including whether she could bear to move out of the room she had been sharing with Dare, or whether she should hang onto every last precious minute with him.

The decision was made for her when he followed her up the stairs and waited barely long enough for the door to close before he wrapped her in his arms.

'I'm sorry, Penny,' he murmured into the side of her neck, the warmth of his breath seeming to travel right through to her soul. 'I should have realised that you're exhausted. It's not like you to be so quiet or to scurry off to bed as soon as the meal's over.'

She blinked back tears as she returned his embrace, and submitted quietly when he undressed her and pulled her nightdress over her head.

'Hurry up with the bathroom,' he murmured huskily before he planted a whisper of a kiss on her lips.

'If nothing else, we can have a cuddle before we go to sleep.'

The last four days had gone by far too fast, with Penny trying to store up every last little memory of her time with Dare to take back with her—knowing they would have to last her for a lifetime.

Now she was sitting strapped into the same seat of the RAF transport plane as before, the same crew welcoming her on her flight back to England as had brought her to Siberia in the first place.

While the plane started to taxi to the far end of the runway she craned her neck to try to catch one last glimpse of Dare, but knew it was hopeless.

Tears began to leak slowly down her cheeks as she relived his farewell kiss, the passion she'd longed for tempered by the presence of their audience.

'Be happy,' he'd murmured as he'd cupped her cheeks in his hands for the last time, and she'd longed to scream out the impossibility of being happy without the man she loved.

But she hadn't.

She couldn't—because she'd never told him that she loved him. Never even dared to mention love because she knew it wasn't what he wanted from her.

A slightly crumpled handkerchief was pressed into her hand and she smiled half-heartedly in the direction of a tear-fuzzy face with a murmured word of thanks.

It would take more than a handkerchief to soak up the tears filling her heart, but this was a long journey and by the time they landed back at the RAF base just outside London she promised herself that she would have everything under control so that no one would ever guess that she'd left her heart in Siberia with Dare.

She'd been doing it for years, she thought with a

self-pitying sob. With her father seemingly intent on ordering her every thought and action, she'd become adept at hiding her thoughts and feelings, just for the sake of peace in the house.

Well, now she had no one to answer to except herself. . .

Her thoughts stopped in mid-train and her hand crept over the deeply hidden evidence of the new person in her life.

Never again would she be making decisions for one. From now on she would be responsible for two lives, and she was going to do everything in her power to make certain that Dare's baby never wanted for anything.

'And in Eastern Russia, aid workers connected with the charity MERLIN are missing, believed dead, when the first aftershock hit the region and a building collapsed near the temporary hospital they were trying to set up,' intoned the voice on the television's early evening news.

Instantly, Penny's head swung round to focus on the screen, dreading what she might see.

She'd kept in contact with the office staff at MERLIN at intervals over the last three months, and they'd told her that the team at Nevansk were starting to hand over their flourishing unit to the enthusiastic staff at the hospital.

They'd also told her that Dare had indicated he was willing to go straight out to wherever the next emergency occurred.

Every fibre of her being clenched tightly in denial as the pictures on the screen showed buildings scattered on the ground, like a children's construction toy pulled apart in a temper tantrum.

'They were members of the advance evaluation team,' the voice continued evenly, not knowing that every word was tearing her heart apart.

'Flew in to assess the emergency medical requirements of the people devastated by the earthquake which struck the region in the early hours of yesterday morning.'

The newscaster's calm delivery of the story was the background to pictures of shattered buildings and shattered lives, but Penny wasn't listening any more. Her hand was already reaching for the telephone, knowing the line was manned twenty-four hours a day.

'Who are the people missing?' she demanded, almost before the phone was answered. 'I've got friends in a team in Siberia. Were any of them involved in the earthquake?'

'I'm sorry,' the unknown voice said soothingly when he'd finished asking her for details about herself to verify her claim. 'We haven't had any communication from the team since we heard that someone was missing so I can't tell you anything further—'

'Please!' Penny broke in frantically. 'I've got to find out somehow. I've got to know if he's still alive—!'

'I've taken your number, and I promise I'll get someone to contact you as soon as we know anything further.'

'Oh, please. As soon as you hear anything. It doesn't matter what time it is. . .'

She had to be satisfied with that, knowing that if MERLIN hadn't heard any news then there was no point trying to contact anyone else.

She sat huddled into the chair closest to the phone with her quilt wrapped around herself, and waited and worried through the night.

Regrets haunted her and she had too many hours to

think of how differently she would have handled things between herself and Dare if she'd known that she might lose him like this.

Honesty made her admit that she'd had a secret hope that he'd realise he missed her and would come back to England to find her, but that same honesty also made her face up to the dishonesty of her actions when she'd left Nevansk.

It was all a matter of duties and rights, she decided as dawn was beginning to lighten the sky outside her window, and she'd ignored both.

She'd had a duty to tell Dare that he'd fathered another child, and he'd had a right to know it. What he would have chosen to do with the information would have been up to him because she had no right to expect him to stay with her just for the sake of the child.

'With my family connections, he wouldn't even have had to worry about supporting the child,' she said aloud into the early morning silence, fighting down the sob which heralded the start of hysteria and biting her tongue.

The phone rang right beside her and she swung round to face it, she stared at it for several fraught seconds—as if it were a rattlesnake poised to strike—before she grabbed for it, nearly knocking it to the floor.

'Hello?' she squeaked almost inaudibly, swallowed to clear her throat and tried again. 'Hello?'

'Penny? It's MERLIN here. I've just come into the office and found your message.'

Penny closed her eyes in gratitude. Thank goodness for a voice she knew.

'Is there any news?' she blurted. 'Have you heard anything about Dare? Is he all right?'

'Yes. He's fine, and he's on his way home. He wasn't involved in the—'

'On his way home?' she broke in wonderingly, almost unable to believe what she was hearing. 'When will he be here? Is he coming on a regular flight or RAF transport? Will he come straight to the office?'

'Whoa, Penny,' The woman on the other end of the phone laughed. 'Hang on a minute and give me time to answer!'

'Sorry,' she said, conscious that her hands were shaking and her pulse was ragged. 'Tell me everything.'

'All I know is that he'll be arriving on a scheduled flight into Heathrow later today. As for where he'll go first, I won't know until he contacts us after the plane's landed.'

'But you will let me know?' she pleaded guiltily. 'I know you're up to your necks in it at the moment, but—'

'All right, all right! Anything for peace!' the woman quipped, and said goodbye.

Penny put the phone down with a clatter and wrapped her arms around herself tightly, hardly able to believe how lucky she'd been.

Now, instead of having to live with the memory of denying Dare the right to know that she was carrying his child, she'd have the chance to put her mistakes right.

And maybe, just maybe, the little voice inside her whispered, he might decide that he wants the commitment of a relationship after all.

It was after midnight, and Penny had reached the stage of biting her fingernails while she waited for the phone call to tell her that Dare had arrived.

There was no point in pestering the office staff any more because she was certain that they would have let her know if there was any further information, and they had enough to do with organising the team to go out to the earthquake region with the first delivery of shelters and medical supplies.

The ring at her doorbell startled her out of her silent rationalising, and she uncurled herself from her seat and wandered across to the door.

At this time of night, the most likely person she would find would be her elderly neighbour, wanting to know if she had any spare milk, so she had no qualms about releasing the catch and opening the door, even in her dressing-gown.

'Hello, Penny,' Dare said quietly. 'Can I come in?'

'Dare!' she gasped. Her eyes raced over him, looking for evidence of injuries. He looked rumpled from many hours of travel and bone-weary, but he'd never looked better to her, and she threw her arms around him.

'Oh, Dare, you're here. . . You're really here. I'm so glad to see you. . .' she babbled as her hands explored him frantically.

'Hey, Penny,' he murmured as he manoeuvred her inside her front door and leant back against it to close it, his arms wrapping right around her as he pulled her against his body.

'Oh, I've missed you so much,' he murmured fervently, but she barely heard him as her heart overflowed with relief and love and sheer gratitude that he'd come to see her.

'Oh, Dare, I'm so glad to see you,' she repeated, barely in control of her tongue.

'I never should have left you the way I did in Nevansk,' she continued, frantic to get everything off her chest. 'I shouldn't have gone away without telling you how I felt, and—'

'And I should never have let you go in the first place,' he broke in fiercely. 'I'd known for weeks that meeting you was the best thing that had ever happened to me, but when I thought you wanted to go—'

'I didn't *want* to go—I *had* to,' she said, using both hands to press against his chest to force him to allow her to step back.

Just those few moments in his arms had given her the courage to tell him everything, and she lifted her chin as she met the dark intensity of his deep blue eyes.

'There's something I need to tell you,' she began huskily. 'Something I should have told you as soon as I found out, but. . .but I didn't have the courage.'

'That you're pregnant?' he questioned softly, his eyes dropping briefly to the slight curve below her waist before they met hers again, full of a searing heat she'd never expected to see again.

'How. . .how did you find out?' she gasped in disbelief. 'I haven't told anyone.'

'Lyudmila guessed,' he said simply. 'And when she saw how miserable I was without you she went and got Yelena to translate for her so that she could tell me what an idiot I'd been to let you go.' He curved a gentle hand around her cheek, his thumb stroking her skin as if he'd missed the feel of it. 'She told me you were in love with me,' he continued huskily, 'and that you were carrying my child.'

'But—'

'Was she right?' he demanded, his voice almost eager.

'Yes, but—'

'I told her she was wrong, you know,' he broke in. 'I told her you couldn't have been in love with me or you'd have told me you were pregnant, but she shook her head. She said there's an old Russian expression which says "a woman's place is in the wrong", and this means you could also have kept the news about the baby to yourself *because* you love me.'

He smiled, and she melted inside, forced to step back into his arms before she collapsed in a puddle at his feet.

'Is it true, then?' he asked softly.

'Yes,' she whispered as she gazed up at him through tear-filled eyes. 'You told me you weren't going to let yourself get attached to anyone in case you got hurt again so how could I try to trap you with a baby?'

'It's only a trap if you don't want to be in it,' he pointed out as he led her across to the chair filled with her abandoned quilt and settled her on his lap, with the down-filled comforter wrapped round the two of them.

'It *did* hurt when I lost Tess and the baby—it will always hurt when you lose the ones you love—but I've been hurting ever since you left Nevansk, knowing that I'd lost you when I could have had you by my side—when I can love you for whatever time we have in the world.'

'Oh, Dare,' she whispered as she gazed up at him. 'I do love you, and I promise I won't try to tie you down. I've proved to myself over the last three months that I can be patient while you're away with one of the MERLIN teams.'

'You can tie me down as much as you like,' he said with a chuckle. 'I've informed them in the London office that I'll still do fundraisers, but won't be taking on any more trips.'

'But what about the earthquake team?' she asked. 'Won't you be involved with that any more?'

'I wasn't involved with that in the first place,' he

explained. 'The first I heard about it was when I phoned to tell them I was taking myself off the ready list and getting the first plane to England. . .

'By the way, you'll be pleased to hear that the missing team members are alive and relatively well—they were trapped in a collapsed cellar and only needed to be dug out.'

Penny murmured her pleasure, but she had more important things on her mind.

'But if you're not going to be flying around the world with MERLIN what will you be doing?'

'I thought I'd apply for a post at one of the London hospitals and wait for someone to snap me up, but in the meantime I hope I'm going to be fairly busy, planning my wedding.'

'Your wedding?' she repeated breathlessly, gazing up at the warmth in his eyes and wondering how she could ever have imagined life without him.

'I'm nothing like the wealthy crowd you're used to, and never will be.' he said, with just a touch of vulnerability in his tone.

'Thank God for that,' she said fervently. 'Those chinless wonders my father's been ramming down my throat have never appealed—not having known the down-to-earth honesty of my grandparents.'

'But they were titled aristocrats, weren't they?' he asked with a frown, temporarily sidetracked.

'Not a bit of it,' she chuckled. 'They were Russian peasants and fiercely proud of their ancestry. It hurt them that when my parents married my father preferred to take my mother's name to hide his humble origins.'

'You didn't answer, you know,' he reminded her when she lapsed into silence, her head cradled on his shoulder. 'You *are* going to marry me, aren't you?'

'Yes,' she said tremulously, smiling up at him. 'Oh,

yes, Dare, I'll marry you. I love you so much. . .I never thought I could be so happy. It feels like magic.'

'Well, it *was* MERLIN who brought us together while we brought a bit of magic to Nevansk so it's only fitting that a little bit of magic should have rubbed off on us.'

She watched him gaze down as he rested his hand possessively over the slight swell of her stomach, and her heart swelled with love.

It almost seemed as if they were surrounded by magic. . .

A sudden wicked thought made her chuckle.

'What?' he asked, raising one eyebrow questioningly.

'Well, I was just thinking. . . You use a magic wand to cast spells, don't you?'

'Yes. . .' he said warily.

'Well,' she continued with a grin, pressing his hand against the slight evidence of their baby, 'if that was a magic spell, did you use a magic wand to put it there?'

'You mean you've forgotten?' he demanded, sounding scandalised. 'In which case, perhaps I'd better introduce you to it again and show you what sort of magic it can perform.'

'Perhaps you had,' she agreed, and squealed when he swung her up into his arms and set off to find her bedroom.

MILLS & BOON®

Medical Romance™

COMING NEXT MONTH

PRECIOUS OFFERINGS by Abigail Gordon

Springfield Community Hospital ... meeting old friends

Rafe was sure that Lucinda couldn't be immune to his charm; after all she was only human; now all he had to do was get her to admit it!

DR McIVER'S BABY by Marion Lennox

Kids & Kisses ... another heart-warming story

Marriage of convenience was definitely the wrong word. Looking after Tom, his baby and his two dogs, Annie thought it must be madness—or was it love?

A CHANCE IN A MILLION by Alison Roberts

It was ancient history. The last time that Fee had seen Jon Fletcher he'd been about to get married and live on the other side of the world. But now he was back and minus a wife...

SOMETHING SPECIAL by Carol Wood

Sam had only one thought on the subject of career women—avoid them at all cost! But getting to know Paula, he was beginning to think he may have been wrong.

On Sale from   **4th May 1998**

Available at most branches of WH Smith, John Menzies, Martins, Tesco, Volume One and Safeway

DANCE FEVER

How would you like to win a year's supply of Mills & Boon® books? Well you can and they're FREE! Simply complete the competition below and send it to us by 31st October 1998. The first five correct entries picked after the closing date will each win a year's subscription to the Mills & Boon series of their choice. What could be easier?

OBLARMOL
AMBUR
RTOXTFO
RASQUE
GANCO

KOPLA
OOOOMTLCIN
MALOENCF
SITWT
LASSA

EVJI
TAZLW
ACHACH
SCDIO
MAABS

G	R	I	H	C	H	A	R	J	T	O	N
O	P	A	R	L	H	U	B	P	I	B	W
M	O	O	R	L	L	A	B	M	C	V	H
B	L	D	I	O	O	K	C	L	U	P	E
R	K	U	B	N	C	R	Q	H	V	R	Z
S	A	N	I	O	O	N	G	W	A	S	V
T	S	I	N	R	M	G	E	U	B	G	H
W	L	G	H	S	O	R	Q	M	M	B	L
I	A	P	N	O	T	S	L	R	A	H	C
S	S	L	U	K	I	A	S	F	S	L	S
T	O	R	T	X	O	F	O	X	T	R	F
G	U	I	P	Z	N	D	I	S	C	O	Q

D8C

Please turn over for details of how to enter ⇨

HOW TO ENTER

There is a list of fifteen mixed up words overleaf, all of which when unscrambled spell popular dances. When you have unscrambled each word, you will find them hidden in the grid. They may appear forwards, backwards or diagonally. As you find each one, draw a line through it. Find all fifteen and fill in the coupon below then pop this page into an envelope and post it today. Don't forget you could win a year's supply of Mills & Boon® books—you don't even need to pay for a stamp!

Mills & Boon Dance Fever Competition
FREEPOST CN81, Croydon, Surrey, CR9 3WZ
EIRE readers send competition to PO Box 4546, Dublin 24.

Please tick the series you would like to receive if you are one of the lucky winners

Presents™ ❏ Enchanted™ ❏ Medical Romance™ ❏
Historical Romance™ ❏ Temptation® ❏

Are you a Reader Service™ subscriber?   Yes ❏   No ❏

Ms/Mrs/Miss/Mr ....Intials ....
(BLOCK CAPITALS PLEASE)

Surname..

Address ....

....

...................................Postcode.........................

(I am over 18 years of age)   D8C

Closing date for entries is 31st October 1998.
One application per household. Competition open to residents of the UK and Ireland only. You may be mailed with offers from other reputable companies as a result of this application. If you would prefer not to receive such offers, please tick this box. ❏

Mills & Boon is a registered trademark of
Harlequin Mills & Boon Ltd.